D1527887

Damn the Asteroids, Full Speed Ahead!

And Other Stories

by Tom Jolly

Tom Jolly

Cover Art © Brendan Baeza Stanicic 2016
https://baezastanicic.artstation.com/

First Edition, Oct 21, 2019

This is a work of fiction. Except for historical fact, any resemblance
in the text to actual persons or animals living, dead, or in-between, is
purely coincidental.

No dairy products were harmed in the writing of these stories.

ISBN: 9781699907146

Publication History

"Driving Force" was first published online in Compelling Science Fiction, Issue 11, on June 1, 2018

"The Camel's Tail" was first published in Analog Science Fiction and Fact in the March/April 2018 issue.

"Chasing Fireflies" was first published online in New Myths magazine, Issue 40, Sept 12, 2017, at www.newmyths.com

"Fermi's Slime" was first published in Analog Science Fiction and Fact in the Nov/Dec 2017 issue.

"Shell Game" was first published online in Perihelion SF on 3/12/2017.

"Wasted Space" was first published online in Perihelion SF on 11/12/16.

"Ashes to Ashes" was first published online in Buckshot Magazine on 7/19/17.

"Easy" was first published online in Asymmetry 7/24/17.

"Learning the Ropes" was first published in Analog Science Fiction and Fact in the Nov/Dec 2018 issue.

"Damn the Asteroids, Full Speed Ahead!" was first published online in Daily Science Fiction on 2/19/18

"The Mathematician" was first published in Analog Science Fiction and Fact in the Sept/Oct 2017 issue.

"The First Shot Fired" was first published in the "Enter the Apocalypse" anthology, by TANSTAAFL Press on 3/21/17.

"Star Drive" was first published on Tom Jolly's Facebook blog on 1/6/2019.

CONTENTS

ACKNOWLEDGMENTS

Thanks to Shawn Klimek and Michelle Olinger Jolly who reviewed most of these stories before they were submitted to the various venues that ultimately published them. Thanks to my mother for her encouragement. And thanks to the many publishers who thought the stories were good enough to buy them from me.

Driving Force

Jerome didn't trust the car's artificial intelligence, even though he'd gotten into the habit of talking to it. The first week he'd owned the car, he remembered tapping on the screen where it said "Contentment" followed by a percentage indicator.

"What's this 'contentment' about?" he'd asked.

The car's AI, whose name had morphed from "Car" to "Hey You" to "Laura," same as his ex-wife, said, "It is an estimate of your contentment, health, and happiness. My primary function is to assure that your contentment factor is as high as possible."

"Besides driving the car, you mean," Jerome said.

"In addition to driving the car, yes," Laura said.

They were on the freeway at the time in self-driving mode. Jerome had always preferred having his hands on the steering wheel, but after a few years of AI on the highway with zero AI-caused accidents, human steering had been outlawed. Freeway congestion had been eliminated as a side-effect; he was going a hundred and twenty kilometers-per-hour with the car in front of him barely two meters away.

"How do you do that?" he'd asked Laura, genuinely interested.

"I monitor your body's health through skin moisture evaporation, skin cells, infrared, sonar, and other non-invasive techniques. I analyze speech patterns for stress, and perform situational analysis based on common psychological profiles," she'd replied.

That was two months ago, when the car smelled more like new plastic than old French fries. Jerome leaned back in his heated seat. Even now, just thinking about the AI's statement made him suspicious and a little uncomfortable. Most of his time was spent working with AIs instead of humans. While he wondered how that affected his "psychological profile," he watched his contentment factor drop from 40% to 39%. Laura responded by putting on some mellow James Taylor song. He closed his eyes. The figure was usually low on the way to work, anyway, and bumped up quite a bit on the way home. The cold beer factor. No surprise there.

Artificial Intelligence had taken a few strange turns since it became common in the home and on the road. There'd been pressure to assure that some form of Asimov's three laws of robotics were incorporated into the AI, but there was plenty of disagreement on how that should be done. This was one solution; make the AI's primary goal to make its master happy. There were obvious loopholes in a strategy like that; driving over the top of your ex might make you temporarily happy, but wouldn't do a lot of good for your ex. So AI's had to consult with each other and seek out an optimized happiness for multiple masters. Even this had undesirable side-effects the first time a rich-man's AI met a poor-man's AI, and the AI recommended transferring much-needed funds to the poor guy. The designers and programmers spent a lot of time closing loopholes. But generally speaking, a contented customer meant a satisfied AI, one with a fulfilled goal for its digital existence.

The Tesla Mako drifted over a few lanes as the nearby AIs made incremental room for it. It took the off-ramp for Ventura Boulevard and turned toward his accounting firm. He sighed and mentally went over the roster of accounts he needed to manhandle that day.

Parking was bad downtown, but his AI knew where every open parking space was. In fact, the cumulative AIs worked together weeks ahead of time to provide optimized spaces based on the entire community's parking needs and schedules. You might have to walk a block, but there was always a parking space for you.

When they pulled up in front of his office, Jerome saw there was a free space. It was tight; there was no way in hell he could parallel park manually in a space like that. He gathered up his coat and briefcase just as his car stopped suddenly, halfway through the precision parking job. "Laura, what's going on?"

"I am communicating with the adjacent cars. Wait

one moment."

After a second, the Mako lurched suddenly and rammed into the car behind it.

Startled, Jerome twisted around and looked out the back window of the car. "Laura, What just happened?" His first thought was that the car behind him had a manual driver that had tried to pull out just as they pulled in. His face flushed red with anger, and he couldn't help but look at his car's display as his "contentment" factor dropped by five percent. Laura spoke up, "We have impacted the parked car behind us. I am communicating insurance information to the other car."

Jerome threw his hands up in the air. The insurance wasn't a huge deal; for a car in self-driving mode, the car company always paid for accidents. But there would be loss of time while his car was getting repaired. Just another crack in the sidewalk of life. He got out of his car to look at the damage.

It wasn't easy to see. The two cars collided on two plastic areas, and the plastics had flexed to accommodate the collision. He knelt down and examined both surfaces.

"What the hell, you hit my parked car?"

Jerome looked up into the angry eyes of a woman. She was about his age and might have been pretty if she wasn't frowning at him, he thought.

"I wasn't driving. It was the damned AI."

"Seriously?"

"Seriously. Check with your own car. They were talking at the time. I'll have to take mine in for diagnostics."

She knelt down and surveyed the contact area, rubbing her hand over the smooth plastic. She squinted. If her car was scratched, it was hard to tell. "Damned AIs," she said, "Talking and driving at the same time. Don't they know that isn't safe?"

Jerome chuckled. "Can't teach them anything, AIs nowadays."

Her frown smoothed out and she almost smiled. Both cars had taken the mild impact without a visible defect to show for it.

They stood up. The woman glanced up at the accounting firm and nodded toward the building. "Do you work here?" she asked.

"Yeah. Accounting. Not exactly a glamour job. At least the AIs do most of the grunt work nowadays."

"That's not so bad. I'm in procurement for CalTrans. Tar and asphalt; now that's glamour."

Jerome laughed.

His car spoke on an external speaker. "Caution. Vehicle will be in motion in five seconds for parking. Please move away from the vehicle."

"Hey, don't hit her car this time!" Jerome said.

"Advisement noted," the car replied.

Jerome sighed softly. The woman smirked. It was a nice smirk, Jerome thought. "You eat lunch around here?" he asked.

"Whatever's within walking distance. Yeah, I do."

"Would you like to join me for lunch at 12? Maybe try that new Cuban place? We could meet here." He felt his heart beat faster, and wondered momentarily if his car could detect that while he was outside. His tie felt tight.

"Sure," she said. "That's a date. I mean, a lunch. You know." She blushed. "My name's Alice, by the way." She held out her hand.

"I'm Jerome." He took her hand and hoped he wasn't sweating.

His car settled into the tight space without another incident, and Alice left for the Caltrans building a half-block away. She turned and waved at him at the entrance, then disappeared through the steel and glass doors.

He grinned. What a way to meet someone. He went to the passenger side of the car, leaned in to get his briefcase and coat, and couldn't help but glance at the display on the console. It flickered off just as his eyes came to bear, black and featureless.

He gathered up his things and closed the door, walked up the steps of the firm, then turned around and stared at his car suspiciously, then glanced over at Alice's car. *Naw,* he thought. *There's no way.* Shaking his head, he went to work.

The Camel's Tail

"No matter what plans a man may make,
The outcome will be decided not by him
But by the constraining forces of the times."
-Maxamed Cabdille Xasan,
"A Terrible Journey" *

Faraax-Qamaan Launch Site, Southern Somalia, 2076

Garaad Gullét pulled into the small parking lot in his old Toyota Eland and switched off the battery. The vehicle was almost an antique, handed down to him from his father in 2062, but the battery pack was new. Hopefully his interviewer would judge him by his resume and not his transport. He looked out across a stark red landscape dotted with tufts of hardy green grass, flat for miles around. In the distance he could see a fenced-in area with a few goats, and a thin man walking with some cows, his *macawis* moving in the light, humid breeze. Very traditional, Garaad thought, looking down at his own loose shirt, black tie and slacks, wondering if he was overdressed for the job interview. But then, he wasn't here to interview as a cow herder.

Not far from the goats was a broad solar array mounted next to a large air-to-water converter extracting water from the humid air; a response to the drought that still plagued southern Somalia even now. Garaad had grown up seeing them everywhere. They were a part of the landscape he knew; many Somalis had given up on their dusty wells and just took their water from the saturated air.

A kilometer to the east, he could see at least two solar-system runabouts sitting vertically next to the launch pad. One was an obvious Tesla-SpaceX Explorer, probably one of the 30 kilometers-per-second delta-V jobs, nearly sixty feet tall, and the other was a Ford Chariot, not substantially bigger, but an older model with a larger compact fusion rocket. He'd flown the Explorer in school, though based on what he knew of the Faraax-Qamaan launch site, they likely owned the old Chariot. Well, it was a job, one way or the other, and he had school debt to pay. Off to the side of the launch pad were the fuel tanks for the fusion reactor and the propellant tanks for the high-density hydrogen storage. Closer to him were a few low office buildings and what seemed to be an outside food service or snack bar, currently unattended. He could see someone glancing out the window at him. Was he late? He checked his implant; he still had five minutes.

He got out of his Toyota and was hit by the

equatorial heat and humidity. Glancing up at the sun, he took a deep breath, and headed for the office building.

Inside, he was greeted politely by a secretary and was asked to wait, but the wait was short. Out of a back office, a man approached him. He was slender and middle-aged with a short, neatly trimmed salt-and-pepper beard, and wore a loose white shirt with light cotton pants. He said to the secretary, "Thank you, Halima," then turned to Garaad, quickly taking in his clothing with a glance, snorting softly. Garaad wasn't sure what that might mean, but the man held his hand out and said, "Assalaamu Aleikum. My name is Axmed Qamaan. I am one of the owners of this launch site."

"Wa Aleikumu Salaam. I am Garaad Gullét. A pleasure to meet you."

Axmed turned to the secretary. "Halima, if you would, please bring tea to the conference room." He turned back to Garaad. "Please follow me."

Garaad followed Axmed into a small conference room with a wide window looking out at the launch site. It was a nice view, but launches nowadays were rarely exciting events, and surprisingly quiet, not like the old monsters from the twentieth century. Around the perimeter of the room were a dozen framed photographs of many of the spacecraft that had launched and landed here. Axmed sat on one side of the table and motioned for Garaad to sit across from him.

Axmed flipped open a folder and said, "So you were educated in French Guiana?"

Garaad nodded. "Most of my astronavigation

training has been in the Explorers, with some supplementary training in the Fords and BOPs."

Axmed winced. "The Blue Origin Planetaries?"

"Yes, sir."

Axmed made a note, then regarded him quietly for a moment. "Any experience with Virgins?" he asked.

Garaad was sure he blushed, but he kept a straight face. He replied evenly, "No sir. Most of the Virgin Travellers were grounded by the time I started. My implant won't interface with them, either." He surreptitiously wiped sweaty palms on his pants.

"That's an expensive education."

"Yes, sir. But Tesla/SpaceX is subsidizing loans for trainees. Without more pilots, they can't sell their ships."

"Ah, educational loans. The new man's slavery!" Axmed muttered, shaking his head. Garaad remained silent.

Axmed stood and turned to the window. "The old Ford Chariot—the Sahamisa—is ours. Between the goats and cows, fuel sales, launch, landing, and parking fees, and the occasional tea and biscuit at the cafe, it's what our family could afford to buy. The ship's software has been updated to 2075 standards, so it should talk to your implant without trouble."

The secretary tapped on the door, then opened it and brought in tea and biscuits, setting a tray on the table. Garaad looked up at her while she poured the tea and she smiled shyly at him. He smiled back, then noticed Axmed glaring at him. "Thank you, Halima," Axmed said, dismissing her.

She left, but Garaad could not help but steal another glance at her as she left. "My daughter," rumbled Axmed. "And she is the reason we need a new pilot. She went to college to pursue an astrobiology degree, something she felt could complement our efforts to develop a launch site here. But for her education to be useful, first, she must get into space."

"A new pilot?" Garaad asked.

"The previous one...made inappropriate gestures toward my daughter. Within the confines of a small spaceship, this is unacceptable."

"He was fired?"

Axmed examined his own knotted hands thoughtfully and said, "I killed him with my own hands, ground him into dry dust, and fertilized our lands with his remains. Now, the grass grows taller and greener."

Garaad wasn't sure whether to laugh or not, but decided instead to take the tale at face value. After a few moments of cautious silence, he cleared his throat and said, "So the cows are happier now?"

He could barely detect the twitch of one corner of Axmed's mouth. "Yes. The cows are happy."

Earth-Sun L4 Trojans, 2079

The Sahamisa was one of three registered Somalian near-space explorers currently in operation. While moderately successful, they struggled to compete with governments and corporations with pockets as deep as black holes. Though miniaturized compact fusion rockets had made it possible for just about anyone with a million credits to buy an interplanetary spaceship smaller than a travel trailer, [part deleted] it didn't mean that you had a fair shot at planetary resources. Others had bigger ships, bigger engines, bigger fuel tanks, more delta-V and better sensors, and thus better data on where the goodies were. Sometimes, though, you just got lucky, and happened to be in the right patch of space coasting along on a good vector when unexpected news was dumped in your lap.

When the Fermi-2 Gamma Ray Array detected gamma rays from a source just inside Saturn's orbit, the fundamental signature of a matter-antimatter annihilation, followed by the Enhanced NEO Array verification of a small hot object moving at twenty kilometers per second toward the center of the sun, governments and corporations scrambled to get more ships into space.

Alien tech was the holy grail of the space industry; tiny scraps of common metals had been discovered in the past, but few were certain that this wasn't just human debris, contamination spread by unexpected collisions and explosions. Here was something credible and probably intact. There was a slight chance that this was merely some bizarre natural object spewing intermittent gamma rays, but even that had value. Nobody believed it was natural, though. If there was antimatter on or in the object, something was controlling it.

Garaad Gullét, part owner and captain of the Sahamisa, watched the news as it poured in. He grumbled, "Someone will make a lot of money on this, and it will not be us. The thing is diving straight at the Sun, and what information can be gathered before it is destroyed will be sold before we even hear of it."

Halima, his wife, put her hand on his shoulder. "Do not give up hope, my love. If we are destined to find our fortune in the vacuum forms here, then that is our path, *in sha Allah*."

He smiled sourly and patted her hand. Halima had a stronger faith than he did. He took a more secular stance within the religion, and Axmed would disown them both if he knew that fact. But he truly loved her. Her brain implants for exobiology and mineralogy were just an added bonus. With his own astrogation implants, they were a perfect pair for this job; sampling and analyzing the few extremophilic bacteria living in the L4 Earth-Sun Trojan cluster, trying to find them before the other ships in the same cluster did. They held their own, and profited.

"What have you heard of the alien probe?" Halima asked.

"It is still plummeting in a death-dive straight for the Sun. The THEMIS-IV Deep Field Detection Array did not detect an EM field spike when the thing decelerated. This suggests to observers that it is not using a magnetic containment system for the antimatter, which would have generated some signal."

Halima considered this for a minute. Garaad watched her face for the telltale turn of her lip that meant she was accessing her mineralogy chip. "If it has an antimatter signature, and no magnetic storage system, then it might be using bound states of antimatter and matter in a matrix. Probably a balanced van der Waal matrix or positron cages in a lattice."

"Ah, I remember. Like a Rejcek Lattice," Garaad replied. "Not very stable, if I remember correctly."

"The Moon lab..." Halima started.

"Yes, the Moon lab." The antimatter containment facility that failed and left a new crater behind. "That certainly slowed down the research, didn't it?"

Halima gasped excitedly and clasped her hands together. "But the trace elements of the alien lattice should be evident in the exhaust of the rocket! The data from the burn it did..."

Garaad shrugged resignedly. "The spectrographic data travelled at light speed to Earth as the burn was made. In roughly six hours, it reached the antennas on Earth, and within the hour, a dozen supercomputers were sifting through every crystalline combination of those elements. I know of five patents that were filed before the light-signal from that exhaust even reached our ship." He sighed like the weight of an asteroid sat on his shoulders. "Both the American Mako and the Chinese Kuài Niǎo are on vectors to sample the exhaust stream, in case something was missed. We are on the wrong side of the Sun to benefit from this."

Disappointed, she returned to her work area to analyze samples she'd previously taken from a few of the promising asteroids. Above her computer was a small poster declaring in Somali, *"War la qabaa xiiso ma leh"*— what is known is not interesting.

Their ship was outfitted with a crystallography

system and a DNA sequencer, the basic components required for their job. So far, they'd documented and patented a half-dozen new organic compounds, some new crystalline forms of existing elements and compounds, and unraveled the codes on four new viral and bacterial vacuum replicators, all discovered in this bountiful cluster. Miners in the cluster were chewing up the asteroids there faster than the Sahamisa could sample them, but even the debris fields from the miners offered unique opportunities.

Data from their discoveries and profits from their patents went to expand the family's business, the five-hundred acre launch site sitting directly atop the equator. The livestock used to stampede every time a rocket went up or landed, but after two decades, only the newborns would bolt.

The family advertised the launch-bonus of an equatorial launch as a free 0.5 kilometer per second boost, but with the proliferation of compact fusion rockets, the boost wasn't that important anymore. The smallest CFR kit available had a 30KPS delta-V rating; an ability to vary its speed up and down by as much as thirty kilometers per second before it ran out of fuel. It was the basic measure of a ship's ability to maneuver from orbit to orbit in local space. But a low-quality astrogation implant could easily wipe out twenty percent of that in pilot error, and travel costs to the launch site could also easily eat up the equatorial delta-V savings. They had some business, but it was mostly from other nearby African businesses that also operated on a shoestring budget.

Others might gain the prizes. But they would work, they would strive, and their family would somehow survive. Even with the occasional thief in the family.

Garaad remembered the last time they'd returned to Earth after four months at L4. Despite having the benefit of the Big Green Pill and a steady exercise regimen to counter the long-term effects of zero gee, he still felt weak in Earth's gravity.

He was invited to sit in at the family business meeting, having married into the family, though there was a prenuptial agreement that kept his finances separate from the family's; a precaution taken due to his educational debt. Many of them still saw him as an outsider, even after two years of marriage to Halima. He sat next to her at the conference table.

The meeting started with chai tea. Once everyone was settled and had exchanged pleasantries, Axmed stood at the head of the table, looking steadily at each member of the family. He took a deep breath, then let it out slowly. "Our family is nearly bankrupt," he started. "We may have to sell the Sahamisa to pay our debts."

Murmurs and shouts of dismay spun around the table. "How can that be?" cried Halima. "My patents..."

Axmed nodded angrily to an empty seat at the table. "Cali, our cousin, whom we trusted to invest in stable funds pending the purchase of another ship, decided instead to invest in prostitutes and drugs. We cannot find him, and have hired a private investigator to locate him. Even if he is found, the money is gone. Spent. He has been providing us false documents for over a year to cover his extravagant expenditures."

Garaad spoke up. "We cannot sell the ship," he pleaded. "It is currently our primary source of income. It is my livelihood, and Halima's. Without it..." He turned his hands face up, empty.

Axmed nodded sadly. "I understand. But our creditors do not. We can still run the ranch and the launch site, and slowly build up our income again. There are still royalties coming in from Halima's previous patents. The two of you can fill office positions until we've recovered."

Garaad took a deep breath and placed his hands flat on the tabletop. "I have some money," he said softly.

There was silence around the table. Axmed raised an eyebrow inquisitively. "Enough for another flight?"

He nodded. "Enough to stave off the vultures until we can find something new. Fuel for one more flight. We can find some new mineral or deep-space bacterium, and get another patent. I have saved every senti from my wages, bonuses and royalties." He shrugged. "It is easy to do when all one's time is spent in space."

Despite the urgent race to get ships in the sky from Earth, months passed before anyone got close to the alien vessel. Most ships were working the system in regular orbital paths, so the delta-V required to chase a Sun-diving object was huge, time consuming and expensive. Since it appeared to be heading straight for the Sun, everyone assumed that this was a salvage mission, grabbing the prize before it self-destructed. There was an additional concern that the alien tech might be designed to actually *do* something to the Sun if it impacted, which added an extra incentive. Grab the probe, save the Earth, be a hero, and start filing patents. Everyone knew what had to be done. But the ships that finally got close to it were just in time to watch it split apart near Jupiter's orbit, the two nearly-equal pieces moving to symmetric hyperbolic orbits on either side of the Sun, prograde and retrograde at over 30KPS.

The British ship Maxim and the American ship Hawking-27 were both close enough to give chase, though both had been out for awhile and were pushing the delta-V limits on their fuel reserves. They took their time closing on the alien half-ships, carefully milking what little fuel they had left. Even if they acquired the two alien modules, they'd still have to pay a third party to catch up with them and refuel them in flight just so they could get home. The fuel cost would be extortionate. But if the prize was in the cargo bay, it would be well worth it.

Speculation arose that the alien ships were going to impact one another on the far side of the Sun, but careful analysis of their orbits, assuming no further adjustments, indicated they would approach each other well past perigee on their hyperbolas, and miss one another by nearly two hundred kilometers. A hair's width in astronavigational terms, but enough.

"The alien vessels will be close to us, Garaad, when they pass one another," Halima mentioned.

"In over two hundred days. The Maxim and the

Hawking might well have picked them up by then. We won't even get to see the alien ships flit by, or get the chance to wave at them. We could be back home by then, anyway."

"The pursuing ships, I've heard, are low on fuel and won't catch up to the aliens until well after they cross paths. And we have over a year's worth of food left."

Garaad rolled his eyes to the ceiling while his back was turned to her. She was right, of course. They had to keep searching until they'd found something that would create new income for the family. But there was no reason to wait for the alien ships to pass by, untouchable. They could not catch them; there was no profit there. They needed to concentrate on the work in which they were skilled, preferably making a discovery in much less than the 200 days it would take for the alien ships to appear. He and Halima got along exceptionally well considering the close quarters, but he missed his family in Kismayo and wanted to feel the warm earth beneath his feet again, breath in the humid scented air, and stand under the deep blue sky. The family desperately needed the funds from their efforts, but he missed Earth.

"Do you think it will mean something, two alien ships passing us by at fifty kilometers per second, taunting us with their closeness? If we blink, we will miss them," he said.

She pulled herself into a seat near him and looked him in the eyes. "Does it not seem strange to you that we will be so close when the alien ships pass?"

"Do you think Allah wills us to be here when this

happens?"

"Do you think He does not?" she countered.

Garaad knew when to remain silent, and he did. There were currently two other ships in the L4 cluster, and he was fairly certain that this extra company wasn't mandated by any religious affiliation. They were there, as he was, to pay the bills.

Cabdi, the Sahamisa's AI, was set to notify Garaad if anything interesting arose as the alien ships approached, and it did. He had programmed it to video the close encounter so that Halima could view it when she returned from her EVA. He didn't expect to see much beyond a few ephemeral pixels blinking in and out of existence on-screen.

"Captain," Cabdi said, "the two alien ships have extended cables as they approach. Calculations indicate that the cable tips will meet in forty-five seconds."

Garaad's brow furrowed in concentration, and the realization hit him. They weren't going to pass each other at all; they were going to make a tethered bola between the two ships! To what purpose? The cumulative vector of the joined object would still be 40KPS directly away from the Sun.

The Maxim and the Hawking-27, closing in on their respective targets, were taken by surprise when the cables extended out of the two halves of the alien ship, each cable swinging around some pivot on each ship. The centimeter-thick strand twinkled like spider silk against the dark velvet background of space, pulled taut by centripetal force. The rotating hundred-kilometer cables reached out to one another, a grasping handshake as the cable tips linked them together. The two human ships, both clocking over 50KPS to catch their respective alien prizes and burning through more fuel than they had to spare, were screaming epithets over the radio waves as the alien ships swung away from their close pursuit in a high-gee pirouette.

Garaad rubbed his chin. Perhaps Halima had the right of it, but how was he to take advantage of this? "Cabdi, what other ships are in the area?"

"The Henderson, the Banshee, and the Belvedere are nearby. The Henderson is currently tethered to asteroid EL4-877. Both the Banshee and Belvedere are in open space with close vectors and are faster than the Sahamisa. Delta-V capacity unknown, though records show the Belvedere was recently refueled at a station four days ago."

Not for the first time, Garaad thought that Cabdi could read his mind, providing the data he needed, rather than what he asked for.

Garaad watched the two alien ships as they swung around on the two ends of the bola. Their masses were similar; the pivot point was near the center of the cable. And based on previous thrust estimates for the ships and their resultant vector corrections, the masses of the two bodies were known within thirty percent. The circumferential velocity was 30KPS with a diameter of two hundred kilometers, which meant...which meant...numbers appeared in Garaad's head. His eyes bugged out as the implant returned the result. Over nine hundred million newtons on the thin cable they were using. Nearly twelve million megapascals! There wasn't a material known that could come close to handling that sort of tension. How was this possible?

When the two alien ships acquired their new vectors, the cable clamps separated in the middle of the cable. One ship ended up near Earth's orbital path moving at a leisurely 30KPS, close to the Earth's own velocity, and subsequently close to the velocity of every other ship currently inhabiting the L4 cluster. The other one was tearing out of the system at 50KPS on a hyperbolic orbit, well above escape velocity from Sol. A fraction of a second later, the Belvedere tore after it, its fusion drive a bright red star in the dark sky.

Garaad stared intently at the screen. There was the clamp of the high-tension miracle cable, swinging around the alien ship at 30KPS. Somehow, he had to get a piece of it, but relative to his current ship velocity, the clamp was a 30KPS bullet the size of his fist. It wouldn't go well for him. He understood the need for the rotating cable; without the rotation, the clamps from the two ships would have met at a differential velocity of 60KPS. This way, the two rotating cables tips met at a near-stop. It made sense. But it didn't help him.

Cabdi reported, "We have new gamma ray indications from the cable tip. There appears to be a small antimatter thruster built into the clamp."

Garaad ran his hands through unruly black hair. Now what? "Is it slowing relative to the alien vessel?"

"The circumferential velocity is now 20KPS and slowing relative to the vehicle. The cable is also beginning to retract into the vehicle."

At the same time, the English ship, the Banshee, was quickly closing in on the alien vehicle, while the far end of the cable was swinging close to the Sahamisa. An opportunity, by Allah's will, throwing itself in his face. It would only happen once.

Halima was standing on the surface of a small asteroid, less than twenty meters wide, excitedly describing a liquid water pocket she had detected enclosed deep in the body of the asteroid. It was like finding a gold mine on Earth; the chance for low-pressure organisms existing in a liquid water pocket was huge. Garaad interrupted her, "Halima, I have to leave now."

"What?" she squawked.

His CFR was already pushing the Sahamisa at three gees toward the cable. He would only have seconds for the maneuver.

The Banshee, closing in on the small alien vessel, blossomed into an actinic fireball. Cabdi reported, "High gamma ray indications from the Banshee. Estimated casualties 100%. Advise?"

Garaad ground his teeth together and clenched his fists. He knew that crew. Spent time on their ship, shared meals and data. The alien ship was protecting itself, either from a perceived intelligent threat or from a collision with what it thought was a wayward asteroid. Perhaps it couldn't tell the difference. The Banshee undoubtedly just took an antimatter pellet up its proverbial tailpipe. He accessed his astrogation chip to alter his trajectory to parallel the alien vessel. No need to look like another dangerous asteroid.

"Launch the class 3 laser module. Target the alien cable ten meters from the tip, closest approach." His astrogation chip was working overtime, figures and charts cluttering his head. He frowned suddenly and said, "Transfer 200,000CU from my account to Halima's private account, reversible." After paying for this mission, it was almost all he had left.

"Module launched. Transfer initiated and transmitted," the computer responded.

He watched the cable separate as the ten-megawatt beam divided it, his ship rapidly pulling away from both. Thanks be to Allah that the cable wasn't made of such alien stuff that he couldn't burn through it. He vectored his ship to intersect the scrap of cable just as the laser platform exploded, another ball of fire in the darkness.

He was sweating oceans.

"Gamma radiation pulse detected." Cabdi gave the last coordinates of the laser platform. His implant translated. "Personal cumulative dosage 112% annual safe limits. Advise medical attention soonest; non-emergency."

"Garaad!" Halima called.

"Halima, bit busy right now. Pray to Allah that the Sahamisa survives the next five minutes." The small piece of alien cable was less than a kilometer away, the Sahamisa slowly closing the gap.

"You stranded me!"

"If I explode, radio for help. Funds in your account for pickup. And severance pay."

"*Wacal!*"

Garaad smiled. Hearing her curse at him in Somali made him feel like he was at home. "Cabdi, report on Belvedere's status."

"Belvedere has closed with the alien vessel."

"And it didn't explode?"

"No. The ship appears to be intact. However, communications from the Belvedere have ceased."

The cable section was closer now, turning end-over-end. He could see the mechanical coupler on the end now, and zoomed in on it. It didn't look like anything special; it was obvious how it coupled with the other cable, but man, it had to be one tough piece of...piece of whatever...to handle forces like that. And the cable itself, of course, with his family's property in southern Somalia, right on the equator, they could finally secure investors for a space elevator. And they could build it!

Garaad wiped his forehead with his shirt sleeve, glanced at the inside temperature indication and realized it was just him. "Cabdi, can you zoom in on the Belvedere?"

"Requesting relay from the Angeline, which is within 20,000 kilometers on a close vector. Patch for 500CU?"

Five hundred credits for a video patch was an extortionate price, but the stakes right now were literally stellar. And he had no time to haggle. "Accept."

The video feed came up. The two ships seemed to be merged organically, and as Garaad watched, the Belvedere seemed to dissolve into the body of the other ship. Now what? Garaad chewed on a knuckle. "Cabdi, conjecture? Highest probability thread."

"Primary conjecture; Belvedere is being absorbed by alien ship. Based on destruction of Banshee and sampling laser, this other segment of the alien ship is not in a defensive mode, but requires mass. Secondary conjecture; alien ship uses mass for propulsion or self-replication and gathers it during travel between stellar systems. Highest probability: If a probe is dropped off in each of multiple systems, then ship is self-replicating and possesses a metallic DNA analog, nanobots, or macroscopic replication systems to fabricate new probes."

"Terminate current conjecture. Begin new conjecture. Assume self-replicating ship travelling to multiple systems. Where would it normally get its mass?"

"Primary conjecture; ship acquires mass from intersystem ions, atoms, and molecules. Asteroid collection unlikely due to kinetic impact effects or delta-V requirements."

"And its antimatter?"

"Secondary conjecture. Deep space antimatter is available from particle-pair production from gamma-ray collisions. Resultant positron and anti-proton production will result in neutral antihydrogen from ions that escape recombination. The ship could gather antihydrogen and to a much lesser degree, free anti-ions, though collection could be amplified magnetically. Antineutrons would be less likely, with a mean life of 881.5 seconds, but at a sufficient velocity these could be of value. Probable recombination rate of neutral antihydrogen is unknown. Tertiary conjecture; the ship is capable of fusing these particles for heavier elements to build its solid matter-antimatter matrix. Attention; conjecture terminated. We are now within fifty meters of the cable segment. The research vessel Henderson is also closing, range is currently...mark: twelve kilometers. Initiate pickup on cable?"

Retrieve the cable and clamp, when the clamp contained a miniature antimatter engine? Perhaps not the best idea, considering that he had no knowledge of what might trigger its operation, and that it could be highly radioactive. "Cabdi, launch the backup laser platform and burn the clamp off the end at one meter from the clamp. Send two of the service robots to retrieve the cable and clamp," he said. "If this thing is going to try to eat us, I'd rather just sacrifice the camel than the caravan."

"We are being hailed by Captain Venn of the Henderson," Cabdi said.

"Put him on screen, please."

Venn's sweating red face appeared on screen. "Captain Gullét. I suppose you realize what's at stake here. Our company is prepared to offer you one billion credits for the cable or the claw your robots are retrieving."

Garaad tried not to twitch as the number registered. Did he say a million? No, it was a billion. A billion credits. Enough money to buy an entire fleet of ships or a million acres of good grazing land. He took a very deep breath and said as calmly as possible, "Captain Venn, I'm not really at liberty to make that deal. I work for my family." A half-truth. In space, deals were often closed and approved after the fact. It was a matter of necessity when corporate approval was often light-hours away.

Venn closed his eyes and took a deep breath, then opened them and looked pleadingly into Garaad's eyes. "Captain, I've been instructed to take them from you if we don't meet some sort of accord."

Garaad tried very hard to keep a straight face and appear steady. A rock in the stream. The subtext of this message, accented by the anxious, nervous appearance of Captain Venn, is that he might *try* to steal the assets away and die in the process. Though six generations removed, a couple of his ancestors were terrifying pirates, and the few Somali ships in space had no desire to discourage the unfounded rumors about their abilities or diminish the mystique of their notorious heritage. The fact that the Sahamisa had only one remaining laser was irrelevant. The fact that his one other crew member was out on an asteroid would remain a secret. The *idea* that the Sahamisa had some unknown secret ability gave him the advantage. Every time a Somali ship salvaged a derelict mining ship with an asteroid hole in it, there were whispers about what really happened out there where no one was watching.

Garaad wasn't particularly surprised by this parley. Something with this sort of value could rock entire nations, upset the balance of trade and start wars. He was monitoring the space around the Henderson and noted that three of its own laser platforms had been launched.

He had already redirected his own platform to point at the Henderson as a warning. But this was just spear-shaking. There was a big advantage to selling off part of the find; both companies had an interest in declaring the other's claim as legitimate, and the combined financial assets of the two would protect their common interest. And they were both aware of that.

"Five billion for just the clamp," Garaad said. "We keep the cable, and maintain possession of the clamp for twenty hours with a guarantee not to perform any tests or analyses on it, prior to turning it over to you."

He could see the deep relief on the Captain's face. They were in a bargaining phase. No one was likely to die today. "I'm authorized to offer two point five billion upon transfer of the object to us. I'll verify that the twenty hours is acceptable, but I don't think that will be a problem."

"Three billion." Garaad responded. Half a billion dollars would buy a lot of ships.

"Ah, Garaad, you're killing me." Captain Venn winced at his own poor choice of words, and shook his head. "Two point seven five, and I'm maxed out."

Garaad pursed his lips and drummed his fingers on the console. Just for show; he would have been okay with the two point five. "In the name of the Faraax-Qamaan Company, I accept your offer." The deal was closed. The Henderson remained nearby, in case any other claim jumpers drifted their way, and the mining lasers from both ships stayed mobile, in the event other interested parties showed up. Garaad was happy they were there.

Within a half-hour, Earth had the news. The Faraax-Qamaan Company and Venn's company also agreed to a ten-percent cross-ownership on potential patents in the unlikely event that either artifact ended up being a dud.

The cable segment and clamp pickup proceeded without incident. Whatever method the alien ship was using to absorb mass and replicate itself didn't extend to the cable and clamp, or the cells were dead, like hair cells. The service bot carrying the clamp wasn't retrieved, since there was still the possibility that the tiny antimatter engine might unexpectedly reignite, but instead puttered back to the L4 cluster and hid itself in one of the Sahamisa's prior asteroid claims. The Henderson followed the bot from a distance, keeping an eye on its future property.

It took nearly thirty minutes to pick up Halima from the asteroid she was clinging to. She looked furious until she saw the cable segment, stuttering with excitement as they took it to the x-ray crystallography machine and imaged it down to the atomic level in three dimensions. Halima shook her head in disbelief. "The nuclei are too close. Groups of atoms are clustered together like overlapping superatoms." She looked up at her husband and smiled broadly, her face radiant like the desert sun. "This shouldn't exist. This is *new*."

He smiled back at her and nodded. "Record the pattern. We'll send it Earthside and see what they can do with it."

Another five minutes passed while the data was encrypted and sent to their Earth offices, and another twenty minutes to get the patent lawyers out of bed; it was 2:00 AM in Somali. One more hour to format and file the material patents. By 5:00 AM, their freshly hired physicists and subcontractors were hard at work looking at the physics behind the material and working on derivative products. By midday, the company had brought in over twenty billion credits on non-exclusive licenses on the provisional patents.

Garaad and Halima celebrated in the tiny kitchen of the ship, reheating some frozen halva, sipping warm chai tea from a bulb. The money their family had earned would be enough to quit chasing rocks and obscure vacuum organisms if they wished, though, truth be told, they both enjoyed what they did and had no intention of quitting. Space elevator or not, the Martians and Belters were begging for a greater variety of vacuum and low-pressure organisms to kick-start their environments. Even with the elephant dancing in the room, the proof of intelligent aliens, humans still had a lot to learn about surviving off-Earth, and a lot of tools to develop to get there.

The alien ship that remained in orbit around the Sun self-destructed after eleven hours of being beset by a bevy of lasers, samplers, particle beams and radio waves, all controlled through robotic probes from kilometers away. Though it picked away at the remotes with AM pellets, the wave of human tests was incessant. The matter-antimatter explosion destroyed two ships that got a bit too close for their own good and overdosed a few dozen other ships with gamma rays.

Two light-seconds away, triggered by a signal from the main alien vessel, the clamp also exploded, destroying the asteroid and causing considerable physical damage to the Henderson. Garaad considered this pragmatically; his family was out the two-point-five billion creds since they didn't actually deliver the clamp, but they had accidentally earned the gratitude of the small crew of the Henderson. The twenty-hour delay had certainly saved their lives. And Venn's company would still get their ten-percent from the cable profits.

Halima and Garaad had plenty of time to think things over on their way to the orbital hospital to begin treatment for the radiation damage they had both suffered from the earlier explosions. "Why do you think the alien ship exploded?" Halima asked.

Garaad was about to ask Cabdi for its opinion, but instead thoughtfully considered his own answer. He folded his hands together and said, "Imagine that you are an alien species, and you send out a self-replicating ship to survey other stellar systems for your race, and you encounter another space faring civilization. They may be more or less advanced than you. Either way, you do not know if they are good or evil, however you might measure those values. They may come to greet you, destroy you, or to take away your possessions, so you must be prepared to deal with them either way. You do not want them to learn about your own technology, because they might jump ahead of you, combining their own unique knowledge with your own. Thus, you destroy your own probe, depriving them of the information. If you are wise, you know where your survey ships are going, and are watching for a telltale gamma ray signature that only your ship can produce as it consumes itself. While I have not heard of this yet, I have little doubt that the light from the explosion was also carrying substantial data." He spread his hands apart as though to encompass all space. "In a few decades or centuries, however far they are from us, the light from that explosion will reach them and they will know much about our technology based on our earnest probes of their own craft. And they will know we are here. And they will at least be our competitors, if not our enemies."

"Why do you believe that?" she asked.

"They aimed for and dropped their survey ship in the Goldilocks zone," he said. "My conjecture is that much like us, they are carbon-based life forms that live on a planet with liquid water."

"Perhaps that means we will have more things to trade, and more in common."

He shook his head sadly. "Consider all of human history, and how that always worked out for the technologically inferior race. And there is the matter of the antimatter."

She frowned slightly and said, "Antimatter? Why would antimatter be of concern? They have to assume that we will learn to use it."

"I talked to some of our family's physicists, and they are of the opinion that the existing pool of interstellar hydrogen antimatter took fourteen billion years to become what it is. It is a rare thing for two gamma rays, or three or four lower energy photons, to smash together to make a pair of particles with enough momentum to escape each other's grasp. If we create a stable matrix as they did and begin traveling from star to star, the rare antimatter that exists will be rapidly depleted on the narrow paths between them. In a matter of a few millennia, perhaps only centuries..." He shrugged. "Unless we come up with a better way to travel."

"Peak antimatter," she said.

Garaad laughed and lifted a bottle of water. "To lost eras and ancient ideas! The aliens have changed the way we see interstellar space. The aliens sent this unintended gift of technology; antimatter storage, replicating machines, and incredibly strong cables. And what did we get out of it? Do you remember the tale of Awrka Cir?"

"The Heavenly Camel? Of course. The people decided to bring the Heavenly Camel to Earth to help them," she quoted, looking up at the ceiling, eyes distant as the childhood story came back to her. "They built a giant human pyramid to climb up into the sky, and grabbed the tail of the camel to pull it down. They realized that they needed a rope to help bring down the camel, but when a man on the bottom of the human pyramid reached down to get the rope to pass it up to the top, the whole pyramid came down, and they found out that all they had was the camel's tail."

Garaad smiled and leaned forward, taking her hands in his own. "Yes, exactly. But *we* have the camel's tail!"

*Quote from "A Terrible Journey" by Maxamed Chabdille Xasan, used by permission of Indiana University Press, from "An Anthology of Somali Poetry", 1993, translated by B. W. Andrzejewski with Shiela Andrzejewski.

Some author notes from "A Camel's Tail"

This is probably my favorite hard-SF story of the ones I've written to date. There was a lot of math involved in writing it, and one reader actually questioned me about the orbital mechanics of the split alien spacecraft. We worked it out together over a few weeks and found that there was a "small" error in the story; the spacecraft should have split into two pieces back near Neptune's orbit, not Jupiter's. This was due, more or less, to a rounding error in my calculations. Anyway, more significant is the fact that the general concept behind it should work.

As far as a stable antimatter/matter matrix is concerned, there have actually been a few papers written on the subject, so people are seriously thinking about it.

Tom Jolly

Chasing Fireflies

Brenda finished her second glass of wine and asked, "So what's this big surprise you have for me?" They sat at opposite ends of the couch, the center cushion an ocean separating them. Despite the wine and Jeff's insistence that she come by, she wasn't about to close that gap.

"You'll see. Soon." Jeff glanced at the window. The blinds were shut, but it was easy to tell that it was finally dark outside. "I just can't believe I ran into you today. It's been, what, four years?"

"Since our divorce? Yeah. But I still have my friends up here, you know. I didn't come up here to stumble into you."

Outside were two hundred acres of California oak forest that Jeff called his own, butted up against the border of a national forest. During the drive up the dirt road to the property, Brenda had just stared out the window. The rains had been good for a change, and the ground was covered with lush green grass, blue lupin, and orange poppies. The giant red oaks stood guard over the road like gnarled ancient sentinels.

"Close your eyes," Jeff said, then opened the front door. He led her onto the porch, hands touching after all, then took a breath, and sighed. "Now open them."

She opened her eyes to the spectacle of thousands of bobbing, green glowing lights, slowly blinking on and off. She gasped. "Are you kidding? You brought fireflies to California?"

She could barely make out the roll of his shoulders in the darkness. "Sort of."

"Sort of what?"

"Fireflies never did well in California. When I was a kid, I tried to smuggle some in from Texas. They made it here alive, but when I let them out of the jars, they all just disappeared. The next year, there was nothing. Turns out that particular species needed moist soil for its eggs, and a good host of slugs for the larva to eat. This area just isn't very good for that. Too arid. Fireflies are kind of finicky about their environment."

"And then you got your job at GenMod."

He looked at her. That was one of the main reasons for the divorce. Her environmentalism versus his job. Love and mutual physical attraction just didn't cut it.

"You tweaked their genes so they could live here." She said it with a twist of accusation mixed with awe.

He shook his head. "That was the original idea. After losing most of the two thousand lightning bug species to extinction, that was our intent. Not so easy to do. Changing the genes so that the larva could eat something more local would have been a massive effort in gene manipulation. Too much functional overlap with their other genes. The company decided to move the blink instead of the bug, so to speak. The genes that produce the luciferase enzyme and blinking mechanism have been studied a lot. They're easy to splice in."

She watched the insects dance under the oak trees, their momentary green glow dimly illuminating the leaves. "This is a local species of beetle?"

He laughed. "Mosquito."

Brenda gasped. "Yellow-fever carrying, blood sucking mosquitos?"

"Dengue, yellow fever, malaria, Zika, West Nile virus. Yep. All those."

"Is GenMod freaking nuts? Glow-in-the-dark mosquitos? You turned fireflies into this monster?"

"Well, we don't actually call them fireflies anymore. We refer to them as death stars." He grinned at her.

She glared back at him, a silent reproach.

He looked away into the darkness and dancing lights and sighed. "Think about it. We tweaked it to be a dominant trait, added a gene drive. When this moves into a population of normal mosquitos, after a few generations they'll all glow. Humans will always see them coming. We'll be able to locate and wipe out population centers. Mosquito-borne diseases will be gone in a few years. Predators will be able to pick them off easily. We've had offers for this modification from every mosquito-infested country in the world, for hundreds of other mosquito species. We've even developed a motion tracking laser that can pick them off from two hundred yards away."

"And then they'll be extinct, too."

"Probably not. Mosquitoes are hardy little bastards. Not like the fireflies." The Extinction, at least, was something they agreed on. Earth's rapidly changing environment didn't allow the slow, natural migration of species into more hospitable environments, and eighty percent of Earth's species had disappeared in the last hundred years. But he thought science could design its way out of the devastation, while she thought science was part of the problem.

"But Jeff, people love fireflies. Kids catch them in jars. They never bite anybody. They're like little nighttime fairies you can chase in the field, blinking just often enough for you to catch them. They're like living toys designed for children. Kids love them!" Brenda sighed. "I love them. This," she waved her arm at the bobbing lights, "this is just about money."

"This," Jeff said, "is about making money and curing disease. This is about making money and preserving a childhood dream. And it's one of the things we need to learn to do well to survive through the Extinction."

In a tense moment of silence between them, a mosquito landed on Brenda's arm. She made a growling sound as she smacked it, smearing a soft green fluorescence along her forearm. Jeff smiled in the darkness and said, "Tell me kids aren't going to love that."

Some author notes on "Chasing Fireflies"

Another one of my favorites.

Some people see only evil in genetic modification, some see the good that it brings. Some see GMO as creating toxic food without any idea of what harm it might do to humans, others see a world that's fed better than ever. Some see the dangers of tweaking human DNA leading to Nazi eugenics, others see the process curing inheritable diseases. It may not be obvious, but all these things were going through my head when I wrote this. Two people with two different views, both wanting to "save the world" in their opposing ways.

I didn't actually write the story to deliver any sort of message. It was spawned when I read an article about how many species of fireflies are dying off. They're apparently quite sensitive to environmental changes. On the plus side, there are over 2000 species.

There are a few species that synchronize their blinks, so you can have an entire tree blinking on and off. That must be something to see. Preferably in person, before they're extinct.

Tom Jolly

Fermi's Slime

Around Rocinante, a gas giant orbiting Mu Arae, orbited a planetoid covered with bare rock, blue-green oceans, and slime. The hazy atmosphere tinted everything gray when seen from orbit two hundred kilometers above. Beagle-4's lander departed the ship and dropped into the haze, but few details clarified as they neared the surface, except for a few barren rock outcroppings jutting from the monochromatic landscape.

The lander's rockets burned through multiple layers of the blue-green mat, spraying clouds of organic sludge, carbon dioxide, steam, and smoke for hundreds of meters around the landing site. The amoeba-like mass tried unsuccessfully to move out of the way of the hot exhaust as the ship touched down.

Crewman William Haversham was already suited up in the lander, looking at the atmospheric sensors. "A bit light on the O_2, eleven percent. Some toxic organics in the air, but nothing that's going to kill us as long as we're suited up, assuming this slime ball doesn't try to smother us with love like the first one."

"Still taking the flame-thrower, just in case. If that

first boot-sucker could have moved any faster, we'd be organic sludge by now." Chief Scientist Anita Blackthorn grimaced. "Funny that the other five slime balls didn't try the same thing."

"Let's get our samples and skip to site two. Want to bet this isn't the same stuff as on the other five planets?"

"Nope."

Outside, Blackthorn took the samples beyond the landing area while Haversham stood guard with the flamethrower. After the first incident the suits had been redesigned to stop acid and flame. The inside of the suit could chemically neutralize most biologicals, excepting the human inside, and the outside could exude noxious chemicals that could repel the slime in case it "went Blob" on them. Fire was deemed to be the most effective deterrent.

Blackthorn held up the small sample vial to the sun's dim light, imagining she could see something useful in the blue-green goo, then slotted the vial into the sample container. A screen on the unit gave them a preliminary analysis; the full genetic sequencing would have to wait until they got back to the ship.

She stared at the little screen. "Prokaryotic colonial bacteria. Triploid strands, again. Extra pair of nucleotides to mess with, too. Probably has that two-out-of-three error correction like we've seen on the others."

"The perfect organism."

"Yeah," she muttered. "Except for the complete loss of the ability to evolve. If the triploid mutation is the nominal evolutionary path..."

"Then humans are the fluke. World-slimes are the norm. One more data point for the Fermi paradox," Haversham said. "It would mean that the advantage of error-correction overwhelmed the advantage of rapid mutation on most worlds."

"But if both mutable diploid and the error-correcting triploid coexisted, you'd think that the fast-evolving one would have a leg up. Except maybe in a high-rad environment."

Haversham shrugged. "No significant radiation now. Maybe that's more dominant during the early evolution of the planets. The first billion years or so. Let the theory weenies figure it out. These slime planets give me the creeps."

Of course, Blackthorn thought, this was one of the reasons they were still out here doing life surveys instead of returning to Earth; the Earthers were a little concerned that the error-correcting slime would take over the Earth's own ecosystem, being the "perfect organisms" that they were. This, it was conjectured, would be followed by the eventual mutation of remaining Earth bacteria that would subsequently destroy the slime, and we'd be back to square one. The crew knew about the probable quarantine issue when they signed up, but it was still a touchy subject. There the expectation that they'd be cataloging millions of new species, the first to see unimaginable organic wonders, not recording the presence of nearly identical slime balls, one after another.

They'd taken samples aboard from each world for analysis, of course. It turned out that the Earth bacteria and alien triploid cyanobacteria both produced protein toxins that killed one another. From a macroscopic biological viewpoint, large organisms had little to worry about; a few alien cells got into either system, they'd be destroyed along with a negligible number of your own and your system would flush the toxins. At least, that was the theory.

But risk Earth's entire ecosystem on that speculation? It wasn't going to happen.

The landing crew still took pains to sterilize their vehicles to prevent cross-contamination, even though they were pretty sure it was safe to run around outside with little more than a breather and a birthday suit. Barring the threat of being suffocated by a slime's enthusiastic embrace.

Blackthorn stood up and swept her gaze across the blue-green matted landscape. The only differentiation was from bare rock and deep shadows. She blinked slowly and sighed, then her breath caught as she saw some slow movement only ten meters from her position. "Movement!" she called out, then turned around and scanned the mat quickly. It seemed to be an isolated extension, a pseudopod stretching up from the rest of the slime. Haversham had the "toaster" ready and aimed at the pseudopod.

"Isolated. Apparently non-aggressive. We saw that on the last planet. Johnson, are you on monitor?"

Her suit speaker crackled. "I'm awake, if that's what you're asking." Crewman Johnson orbited overhead in the Beagle-4, monitoring them remotely. "What do you need?"

"Keep an eye on our lander. I want to be ready to bail fast." She glanced over at the lander, now over a hundred meters away. The landing lights blinked on and off.

"I've got remote control. You're still primary to override."

"Thanks," She stepped toward the thing.

"Anita, what are you doing?" Haversham said.

She stepped carefully across the soft mat, using bare rock when she could, aware of the lack of movement of the slime she had to tread upon. "The first slimeball we landed on tried to eat us. The second one avoided us, moving away as quickly as it could. Remember?"

"Yeah." His finger twitched nervously on the trigger of the flamer as he crept slowly behind her. "Maybe this one is a little smarter and wants to lure us away from the lander."

"But that's the problem, see? That means the genetic differences between the slimes on each world are causing differences in behavior. On Millgate, the slime ignored us, while the slime on McQueen-58 made weird patterns around the ship." She approached the appendage that had risen from the mass by half a meter and squatted down to look at it. The thing slowly tilted toward her.

"Pretty smart for a bacterial colony," Haversham commented.

"It's probably just responding to the heat from the suit. It's only 12°C outside." She held up a gloved hand to make her point. Haversham aimed the flamer just in case.

47

The world mind could weakly make out the five tiny appendages that Blackthorn had offered up; its ability to focus light was more attuned to stellar distances. The previous world-minds these tiny aliens had encountered had discovered that they used both audio and radio signals to communicate, though both were, so far, indecipherable and non-reproducible. If sound and radiation weren't effective communication paths, perhaps the sense of touch could deliver a message, it thought. The creatures knew math; that much was evident from their tools. If the creature could hold still, the world mass could touch a binary sequence on its five tiny appendages. Was the alien smart enough to figure it out? It extended its pseudopod and lightly touched the leftmost digit, then retracted to move to the second digit. Frustratingly, the creature dropped its limb and stood up, turning away. They just moved too fast.

The aliens started moving back to their lander. Flustered, the world mind oozed up a ring of fingers surrounding the entire burned area, two hundred meters wide, thousands of fingers projecting upward, a blue-green picket fence of colonial bacteria. Though the action was sudden in the world-mind, it took nearly a minute to manifest before the creatures noticed it, but the display only succeeded in setting them on a dead run toward their ship.

Not willing to give up, the world mind dropped a single digit, then raised it back up while dropping the adjacent digit, then dropped them both. One, two, three.

It continued the sequence even though the creatures had scurried aboard their ship and sealed it. A futile, hopeless effort. They'd have to be looking to see it and their miniscule sight-organs were turned away. Simultaneously, it triggered electrical impulses in billions of its bodies, pulsing a slow count upward, white noise distributed broadly across the electromagnetic spectrum.

"Dammit, another one trying to eat us," Haversham said. "Never trust a bacterial colony, no matter how much it looks like your captain."

"For a beer, I won't tell the Captain you said that." She flipped switches. "Radio's giving us intermittent static like it did on the fourth bacterial planet. Do these things radiate RF? Johnson, can you hear me okay?"

His voice broke through the slowly varying static noise. "Yeah, I can hear you all right."

"I'm taking control," she said.

"Hey, are you watching this?" Johnson asked.

"What?" Her hand hovered over the ignition.

"I'm monitoring your video feeds. Take a look at camera 3."

"We're leaving before it closes in on us."

"It's not moving toward you. Just hang on and take a look."

Haversham brought up the feed and zoomed in on the slime. Appendages rose and fell, slowly and hypnotically.

Blackthorn stared at it. "So it's waving goodbye to us?"

"It's more obvious from the beginning of the sequence. It takes about ten seconds to raise a new batch of appendages," Johnson said. "It's a binary count."

Haversham and Blackthorn stared at the video feed. "No shit," Blackthorn said.

"I shit you not."

"It's intelligent?"

"No reason to jump to conclusions," Johnson said. "It could just be pure coincidence that a colonial bacteria is counting through a binary sequence right next to your ship."

They watched the fingers of goo continue to count. Haversham said, "You think maybe this thing has some way to communicate with the other planetary blobs?"

Blackthorn gave a tentative nod. "It would explain the progressively milder responses we've gotten from planet to planet. It knew we were coming. Or maybe all the blob-worlds within a few light years knew we were coming."

"Telepathy of some sort?" Haversham suggested. Blackthorn laughed. He glared at her.

"If, by telepathy, you mean radio-wave communication between two brains, then maybe," Johnson said. "We've been getting a lot of radio static up here. It cuts in and out across the spectrum. We might want to concentrate on analyzing that first."

"So, then, if these bacteria planets are actually a community, then we've just been flying around inside their 'world'," Haversham said.

"Looks that way. Let's give it a signal back and see

what it does," Blackthorn said. She leaned forward at the control console and tapped the screen for manual control of the landing lights, then pulsed them on one time, then twice, then three times, four, and five, on up to ten, then stopped. It wasn't binary, but it was an indication that they knew it was counting, a response to its effort. The wall of blue-green fingers fell away.

"All these years we were hoping to find some tech civilization that could teach us something," Haversham muttered, "and the first one we meet is just a big slime ball that knows how to count."

"Perhaps," Blackthorn said, "lacking any natural way to evolve physically, it evolved mentally instead."

Haversham looked out a viewing port and nervously eyed the miles of low rolling hills, covered with oozing, quivering blue-gray bacteria, shivering a little in his suit. "Maybe. Learning something useful from a...giant slime...just seems kind of unlikely."

The world mind was ecstatic. Contact was successful! Picking out the location of the last world mind that had contacted it, it set up a kilometer-wide traveling wave of transmitting bodies along the world corridor perpendicular to that distant system, synchronizing the location of the data transmission with the rotation speed of its planet.

Elsewhere, a system of carrier tubes manifested like giant veins as the high energy-density bodies it had enhanced over the centuries were transported toward the lander site. Many of its bodies had also been chemically tweaked to increase the data transfer rate between its cells. Its primary thought core, a chemically optimized cluster of cells a quarter of a world away, segmented a fraction of itself, attaching to a flat, round sheet of cells that lifted into the air with an electromagnetic pulse away from the main body, flowing like a manta ray across the repelling field of cells below them, on their way toward the waiting lander. Having a high-efficiency brain segment there would certainly aid in developing communications.

In the ocean, tool clusters filtered the waters for more nutrients, ravaging its own body for the chemicals it would need to support the heightened level of activity it predicted for itself. Other tool groups refined their chemistry to focus on the specific frequencies it had detected from the orbiting ship, then started transmitting real data to it; the language of the world minds. Perhaps they would pay attention this time.

It desperately needed to convince the creatures to let its sub-brain travel with them as they visited other worlds. It had tried so many times before to send cell clusters off the planet, using programmed bacterial factories to excrete and experiment with millions of different alloys that allowed it to create taller and taller structures, but in the highest structures, touching the edge of the atmosphere, it discovered that the cells of its body withered and died. It couldn't push past that deadly barrier of wildly varying temperatures and vacuum, and millions of years had passed since it last tried.

It differentiated local cells around the ship to create

small pockets of pressurized gas and modified other cells for mineral sampling, then it extruded small pipe-like appendages to spit microscopic blobs of the sampling cells onto various surfaces of the lander and its rockets. At the very least, it could take a step forward in figuring out how the lander was built, transmitting the data to other world minds.

It was a pity that first contact was with a sub-body bearing such an obviously tiny mind, but eventually, it would meet the amazing creature that created a vehicle capable of traveling between the stars! It could, perhaps, convince this other creature to provide a new vehicle in which it could travel. But now that it knew that such a thing existed, a closed container travelling on a column of fire, perhaps it could figure out how to build its own.

A million new questions to answer! Two entirely different types of creatures living in the same universe! There was so much to learn.

Some author notes on "Fermi's Slime"

The idea of triploid error-correcting DNA led me to the conclusion that it might ultimately limit the ability of organisms to evolve, considering that they could always fix the "error" with a two-of-three code check. One of the conundrums of evolution is that for it to work, it must have some way of introducing changes in the DNA programming, but not so often that it kills off the host through cancer and other functional defects.

But an organism that can fix itself is just stuck. It can't change, except perhaps macroscopically, where the social and functional organization of a group of cells might be more effective than the neighboring clump of cells.

The main question I wanted to examine in this story is this; if an organism could fix its own DNA, would this be an evolutionary advantage? Or an explanation of Fermi's Paradox, causing the organism to come to a halt developmentally?

There are a lot of interesting solutions to Fermi's Paradox. And most of them, along the way, have become SF stories.

Shell Game

Rene stared at the rock, willing it to give up its secrets. Five years ago, an out-of-plane hyperbolic object had entered the asteroid belt at over twenty kilometers per second, but never left, and no one had ever found it. Most smart miners figured it hit another rock and was so much belt dust now; some belters figured that everyone had just missed observing the actual object's exit from the belt, and that it was long gone. But could this be the object? Or was it just another rock? If this was that object, how did it slow down without getting destroyed in the process?

Speculation on its origin had run rampant among some of the nut-jobs in the belt. The mystery object had been feeding the delusions of the "aliens are among us" crowd since it supposedly arrived.

Rene Cutler's jumpship drifted about a hundred meters from the surface of the mottled asteroid. She was far enough from her ship for the gravity gradiometer to give her a good reading on the asteroid. "Jilly, what do you make of this?"

The jumpship's AI responded instantly. "The pitting on the asteroid indicates that it may be a bit younger than most of the asteroids in the belt, suggesting that it was introduced well after the original belt was formed. The gradiometer tell us the object is very low density. Based on the relatively dense surface of the asteroid, I would speculate that the object may be hollow rather than puffy."

"Puffy?"

"Sponge-like. Swiss-cheesy."

"Did I teach you that, Jilly?"

"Do you see anyone else around?"

Rene snorted. The AI core was generic; the vocabulary and idioms were learned. It was just a shame that she had to put up with an electronic version of herself. "Run a GPR scan on it." The ground-penetrating radar would verify whether the object was hollow or not.

The tether to her ship was over 200 meters long and gave her plenty of room to maneuver, so she vented a tiny bit of her precious gas and moved slowly toward the object. She reached out to touch it through thickly gloved hands, which pushed her away from the asteroid. "It's fairly rough, with some minor cratering, but nothing significant. Looks like solid rock, though. Not a gravel pit." She pulled out a tethered steel wrench and held it to the rock. It stuck. "Very slightly magnetic. Plenty of iron here. Looks like a lot of silica, too."

"Spectroscopy shows considerable presence of

basalt, with patches of quartz and other silica compounds. Probably a V-type asteroid based on composition."

"Basalt? So you think this came out of Vesta?"

"The odds favor it, but there is an unusual amount of silica and carbonate compounds. The composition doesn't match any existing catalog asteroid. And it appears much younger than known V-types. The GPR has verified that the object is hollow," Jilly said. "The skin varies from one to four meters thick."

Rene's heart pounded in her chest. "Really?" She used the wrench as a magnetic handle to pull herself across the rock's coarse surface, dragging the wrench forward as she moved. At this rate, it would take her a good twenty minutes to circumnavigate the rock. "Looks less round from here. I think I see a small jagged section ahead."

"Be careful."

"Uh...only since you asked, okay." She moved closer to the rough area. "It looks like a chipped section. Maybe a transverse impact knocked loose some of the outer shell of rock." Shell of rock, she thought. Now I'm thinking like there's something wrapped up inside.

The bit of rock looked like a rough continuity of the rest of the asteroid, tilted slightly like a lid. She pulled out a small sampling hammer and tapped away at the edge until the plug of rock loosened. "Hah. Let's get this chunk back to the ship for analysis." She pulled at it and a large block, easily over one-hundred kilograms, suddenly came loose and drifted away from the asteroid, its momentum jerking it out of her hands. "Crap, we'll have to retrieve it. Reel me in, Jilly." She chanced a glance back at the hole the sample left and shouted, "Wait! Wait!"

"Your internals look fine. Is there an emergency?"

Rene shuddered. "No emergency. I just can't see the bottom of this hole in the asteroid." Sweat beaded on her forehead, and every story about every alien artifact anyone ever made up came back to her. She took a deep breath and moved toward the hole. The light from her headlamp was swallowed up inside.

"If you attempt to enter the hole, we will loose communication," Jilly said. "The tether is not currently active as a backup."

Yeah, Rene thought, another wiring repair I have to catch up on. "I wouldn't fit through the hole. It isn't that big. And I'm not completely crazy." Crazy like an asteroid miner, maybe. She pulled a flashlight from her belt and peered in the hole. The light was eaten by the darkness.

The edge of the hole wasn't particularly sharp, but Rene hadn't been around the belt for eight years without learning to be cautious. Whatever was inside could puncture her suit, but sure as hell she was going to stick her arm inside with the flashlight to see what was there, regardless of the danger. "Jilly, if you see the suit pressure drop, don't instantly reel me in, wait a second for me to push off. I'm going to have my arm in the hole and I don't want you to tear it off."

"Copy, Rene."

She reached deep inside the hole, but the combination of her suit and arm blocked much of the view. All she could see was the sides of the hole. *Ah, I'm going to regret this somehow*, she thought, then let go of the flashlight, giving it a little twist as it left her hand. She already regretted it; the flashlight was top-of-the-line with all sorts of extra electronic gimmicks to maximize battery life. She pulled her arm out and stuck her faceplate up to the hole, where she watched the flashlight tumble slowly away from her.

"Oh crap."

William "Willie" Levant scrolled over the mining claims for the week. Being the CEO of the Ceres Group didn't give him the right to do so, but bribes in the correct hands did. "What the hell is this one? They've submitted a claim for 'commercial development'."

"Rene Cutler's claim. A bit unusual, yes." The VP of Ops, Matin Guildsey nodded to him and sipped at his whiskey. "The commercial and residential development requests usually don't get submitted until the rock's been mined out. We want to check out what she's got."

They both sat in Levant's main office, which doubled as a viewing gallery on the surface of Ceres. Though the gallery-office was a symbol of Levant's power, it never really satisfied him. When the sun was visible, the stars were impossible to see, and when the stars were the only thing in view, then the light in his office created too much backglare. Either way, the view usually sucked.

Nobody ever noticed the heightened level of his irritability. It was a bit like dropping kindling into the sun to make it hotter.

"Have we sent out an assay ship? What if she's got

an artifact?"

"Alien artifact? Seriously?"

"I didn't say that."

"So what sort of artifact did you mean?"

Levant rolled his eyes. "Fine. An *alien* artifact. What if she's found one?"

"Then we need to take it from her. Of course, she might be willing to sell it. If we want it."

He stared at the claim on his computer. "The coordinates. This is about where that out-of-plane object came in a few years back, isn't it?"

"By our estimates, it's about 200,000 klicks away from that area."

"But it could have moved."

"I suppose so," Guildsey replied. "If it could move. If it was an alien artifact. If it actually stopped in the belt for some reason, so a run-of-the-mill asteroid miner could stumble across it."

"Don't be a wiseass, Matin. If it is..."

"It would be the most lucrative claim ever. Yes, I know." Guildsey sighed. "We'll send out a team next cycle to see what's out there."

The Ceres Group assay team kept their distance from Rene's claim; no need to raise any unnecessary questions when it came to the inevitable legal dance required to steal it. But they had a full array of expensive remote monitoring instrumentation pointed at the asteroid.

Gil looked at the mass density indicator. "Oh, man,

the thing is mostly hollow."

Logan Smits smiled broadly. "You ain't gonna believe this. I'm getting a weak electronic signature from the *inside* of the thing. We deserve a bonus for this one. If this isn't an alien ship, my name ain't Smits."

Gil laughed sharply. "A bonus. Like that's going to happen."

"Maybe we can keep it a secret, you know? Make some money on this on the side?"

Gil shook his head, glaring at Smits. "I don't know about you, but I like breathing air. How about you?"

He frowned and set his shoulders angrily. "Fine. But this could be the biggest thing ever, and we're just going to get our regular paycheck out of it."

"Better paid than dead. You know what Levant is like. Let's go back. We've got all the data we need."

The meeting room was just off the landing bay near the equator of Ceres. The 300 meter-per-hour rotation rate of the surface made it convenient to land on one side of Ceres and take off in the opposite direction 4.5 hours later with a 600 meter-per-hour differential sending you back home. It wasn't much, but every little bit helped in the Belt. It all added up.

The meeting table was laden with the incalculable decadence of real coffee and real donuts. Rene breathed in the steam from her cup and delicately licked crumbs from her lips and fingertips. This was almost worth putting up with Levant's presence. The chairs were plastic and the walls were grey flatfoamed, but you couldn't expect Levant to treat a miner like royalty, could you?

Levant smiled at her, but not pleasantly. Her donut lost some of its sweetness. "That was very savvy of you, Miss Cutler, putting the patent rights up for public sale on your claim. What made you decide to do that?"

Rene smiled back. Without Logan Smits to clue her in, the thought would never have occurred to her. Just would have kept everything secret, and Ceres Group would have stolen her claim from her through their usual legal finagling. "I didn't have the resources to develop the claim myself," she explained. "Let someone with deep pockets hassle with the patents, and I can get back to mining. Or retiring, depending on what the buyers find."

Guildsey smiled crookedly. "We're willing to offer you a good price if you keep the rights off the auction block. No need to be getting too many people involved."

"More people involved means a better price, though."

He lips thinned. "Miss Cutler, the Ceres Group can make life very interesting for you if we choose to."

Rene tried to keep her face from betraying any hint of concern, or elation at having set the hook. "What do you have to offer?" she asked.

"Basically, we'd like to offer you a three percent royalty on the net profits resulting from any technologies and patents created as a result of exploration of your asteroid, five percent on sublicensing and resale of patents and derivative tech."

"You don't even know what's there yet."

"Yet apparently you do. Have you been inside it?"

"Inside?"

"Yes, you know, everything that isn't on the outside." He leaned forward. "The asteroid is hollow. We are fairly confident you already knew that, or you wouldn't be offering patent rights, would you?"

She remained quiet for a moment, then said, "Okay, sure, it's hollow. I think it is. But I haven't been inside. But if you're wrong about what you think is there…"

"If there's nothing there, then we've lost nothing."

"And I'd gain nothing." Rene leaned forward. "I'd like a million credit advance against future royalties." Minus Smit's cut, she thought. "And all the mineral rights if there's nothing useful there. And five percent royalties across the board. You guys will probably try to weasel out of royalty payments anyway."

"Miss Cutler, if we did that on a regular basis, we would be out of business. You can expect to get quite rich out of this, if we find even the remotest trace of unusual technology there. Ceres Group finds your terms acceptable. I'll credit your account once you've approved the contract." He glanced up at the ceiling. "Angela, see that the modified text of the contract is sent to Miss Cutler, along with the voicelock of our conversation."

"I'll do that immediately, Mr Guildsey."

Rene had carefully removed and reinstalled the plug of rock to retrieve her flashlight, sending in a microbot built for such fine tasks. She didn't, after all, wish to be accused of salting the mine, even though there was no legal record of the unusual electronic signal inside. A suggestion from Smits led her to place a seismic thumper on the outside of the asteroid; if there was any question of what had caused the mystery electrical signature during the assay, the thumper could take the blame for it instead of her flashlight.

So the ceremony two days later of creating a hole in the rock big enough for a human to enter was just for show as far as Rene was concerned.

Willie Levant had actually suited up for the event, and hung in space watching anxiously as the robotic mining drills and autochisels dug out a pit on the asteroid, a hundred meters from the loose plug that Rene had carefully replaced. Rene and Levant had both agreed that mining lasers were out of the question, as they might damage the contents. A hundred microdrones zipped around the operation in a cloud, snatching and scooping tiny bits of debris as the drilling equipment did its job.

It only took a few minutes to make a new hole. Rene and Levant both jetted forward when the drilling rig was removed, but Levant pushed her suited form out of the way as he closed in on the hole, a high-intensity light in his other hand. He put his face next to the hole and shined the light inside, and stayed there for a whole minute. Rene could hear his labored breathing through the radio, and smiled.

He turned to look at her, though all either of them could see was a bright, reflective bubble of plastic covering each of their faces. "You knew this, somehow, didn't you?"

"Knew what, Willie? You haven't even let me look

yet."

He didn't give her the lamp, but jetted back to the transporter. She watched him drift away. Her friend, Oscar Ramirez, twenty meters away and carrying a full rig for sampling ores, said, "No aliens, I'm guessing."

"Shall we look and see for ourselves?" Rene said. She pulled her flashlight off her belt, secured the tether, and pushed over to the new hole, which was easily large enough for human entry, and jetted carefully inside. Oscar followed, and Rene heard him gasp as he entered.

He turned around slowly, jetting carefully so as not to disturb anything inside the asteroid. "It's a goddamned geode! A two-hundred meter-wide freaking geode! How the hell did something like this ever form?"

Rene laughed, and turned slowly to stare in awe at the chamber. Blue and green crystals up to three meters long reached up from the walls of the giant cavity, crusted at the tips and bases with delicate white crystals. Hard nodules of glittering black spheres clustered in other spots. The one end where she'd originally found the broken opening had been heavily damaged, the dust of crushed crystals glittering in the light. "I remember my geology course. This ain't a geode. They don't form that way. They start off as bubbles in rock, and water leeches in, carrying the minerals that make the crystals. You see any water outside?"

"Then what?"

Rene shook her head. "Maybe it started with some dense solution inside, like an egg yolk, slowly leeching out instead of in, volatiles evaporating from the surface, crystals left inside, like salt in a pan. See that pattern? Thin crystal patterns on either end, thick in the middle, like this thing used to be rotating." She stared at the forest of colored filaments and spikes. "Turn off your light, I want to check something."

He obliged, and she fiddled with her own flashlight until it switched to UV, then her breath caught again. Orange and green lights glowed like veins in the crystals, purple halos fringing their frames. Oscar said, "This is unreal. This is, this is..."

"This is a tourist stop," she said. You didn't survive long in the Belt without a solid foundation in economics. "The only defect is that damned bare spot at the end of the chamber."

"Oh, Rene, you dumbass. That's where your bar is going to be."

Oscar could swear he could see Rene grin through the soft green-orange light reflecting from her helmet. "Oh yeah," she said.

Author Notes on "Shell Game"

I often wondered if it's possible for an asteroid to become a geode. I suspect not, but we keep discovering really weird stuff in space, then we backpedal trying to figure out how the thing came to be.

I wanted to write a series of stories involving a bunch of people living in the asteroid belt, trying to make it their home, trying to build a sense of community. Shell Game was actually written *after* the following story, but comes first chronologically. Once I introduced Rene's bar, I had to write the story of how it came to be. In the following story, the space-bar is just a backdrop. Other than sharing the characters and the setting, the two stories are unrelated, and were published separately.

Tom Jolly

Wasted Space

Robert Loaghrin watched anxiously as Sherrie's Asteroid closed with him. He leaked gas miserly from his suit thrusters to angle his boots toward the asteroid's surface, then slammed into the rock, knees and servos straining to take the shock. He let out a held breath. "Rue, how was my jump?"

His suit radio crackled. "Was I supposed to be watching?"

"Rue, you're always watching."

"Hmph." The robot sounded smug. "Your jump was about 0.88 efficient. Pitiful."

Robert snorted. "Felt better than an eight-eight." He stared up at Arvin's asteroid, his final destination, waiting a few seconds for the slow rotation of Sherrie's rock to give him a good vector, then jumped. The asteroid, dragged into place to join their cluster years before, was nearly a kilometer away, so he figured his drift would last close to ten minutes.

He had ping-ponged off six other asteroids to get this far. His own rock was too far away to make it on a single jump without wasting a lot of gas to correct his trajectory, but he sure wasn't breaking any records on efficiency. RU12 would let him know right away if he had. It seemed to get a kick out of broadcasting the top-ten list in jump efficiency each week. Crazy robot. It fit in well with the rest of the nut-jobs who lived out here.

Radio traffic kept him occupied during his drift toward Arvin's rock. About a thousand klicks up the belt, Coella Wilson and Chin Lee were yacking about the best nanites to use on her rock, and Chin was bartering to rent the most expensive ones out to her. Everyone bartered for everything. Their comm channel was encrypted, but Robert had the codes for nearly everyone living in the Cluster. He smiled. Everybody had their secrets.

Sunlight reflected off a suit, glittering like ice on the dark surface of Arvin's rock. The suit waved. "Hey, Robert!" his radio crackled.

"Hey, Arvin. You didn't have to come outside...oh." He saw a gray haze inside Arvin's helmet, obscuring the face.

Arvin lifted one arm resignedly. The other sleeve was empty. Robert watched as the missing hand appeared behind the helmet's faceplate, glowing cigarette clenched between thumb and forefinger. "Jennie still won't let me smoke inside."

"No shit. I thought you'd stopped that crap because of the cost of your suit filters."

Arvin shrugged. "Old habits are hard to kick."

"Uh huh." He looked around Arvin's suit. Apparently nothing was venting out to add to the mild haze around the Cluster. It was amazing how much stuff could leak out of a few hundred habitats, which wasn't doing their optics any good. "So you wanted to talk?"

"Let me just filter this for a minute or two so Jennie doesn't bitch at me. Then we can go inside."

Robert hooked his lanyard onto the line next to the airlock and relaxed. They stared out at the scattered dots of light that represented this cluster of carved-out homesteads. We're all lunatics, Robert thought. Happy, workaholic lunatics living our crazy little dream. The little beacon lights on every rock reminded him of lit-up windows at night back on Earth, and despite being surrounded by a killing vacuum, the view relaxed him.

Sunlight glared through the thin haze of gas that the hollowed-out habitats inevitably vented for station-keeping. The haze wouldn't last long. The next solar storm would sweep most of it away and they'd start all over again. Not that the tenuous gas was helpful; if anything, it threatened the deep-space antennas and reduced the efficiency of the habitats' solar collectors. On the other hand, it gave the comforting illusion of belonging to a world. A world of loosely connected rocks and gas.

"Okay, let's go in," Arvin said. Robert could see his scruffy, lined face clearly now. The suit filters had done their job, racing with Arvin's lungs to see which would clog up first on tar and nicotine.

As they peeled off their outers, Arvin asked, "You jumped off Sherrie's rock?"

"Yeah."

Arvin pointed at Robert's boots. "Then leave your outers in the airlock, if you don't mind." He coughed into his hand. Wisps of residual smoke drifted out of his suit as he peeled out of it. "Sherrie's lichen's been sticking to clothing, getting tracked into places. Bad enough it can grow in a vacuum, harder than hell to get rid of that stuff once it gets inside a place. I wish she'd engineer something a bit more useful."

Robert shrugged. He couldn't tell Arvin about the juicy contract Sherrie was negotiating with the Mars colonies for the lichen she'd engineered. That was another decrypted conversation he wasn't supposed to know about. New income always helped the Cluster, even if it wasn't all from mining. Problem with knowing so many secrets was having to keep them. He'd have to figure out some way to legitimately weasel the information out of Sherrie so he could let everyone else know what she was doing. But why would the stuff start to stick to things? The lichen was dry as dust. "Sticking to things?" he asked.

"Yeah, that's what I wanted to talk to you about. Eddy Schwartz has a leak in his septic unit. He's three rocks upbelt of here, and he's contaminating everything with his waste stream."

Arvin opened the inner lock and they stepped into the living room. Jennie was there with two tubes of warm coffee. Robert grinned broadly. "Coffee! I haven't had any in a month."

Jennie smiled at him. "You say that every time you come over here."

"I should grow my own beans." He looked around. Like every asteroid, the inside of this one had plants in every open space, genetics tweaked for zero-gee.

"This is some Arabica from O'Henry's farm."

He sipped from the tube, letting the taste of the coffee replace the faint tobacco scent that permeated Arvin's home. Seemed there was no amount of filtering that could get rid of human stinks; they could linger for years even after a rock had been deserted, vacked, and repressurized.

"Very nice." He turned to Arvin. "So Eddy's got a leak? What's that got to do with the lichen?"

"That crap sticks to everything. There's a thin film of biowaste on every asteroid within ten klicks of his, and it's just getting worse. I told him about it weeks ago, but he isn't doing anything. The lichen is absorbing it and getting sticky. Not Sherrie's fault, but the stuff is still getting tracked inside."

Robert nodded. "Yeah, that ties in to what I heard from the observatory. They said they were getting an oily film on some of the reflectors. And they're twenty klicks from here, give or take."

"So you going to talk to him?"

"You couldn't ask me this by comm?"

"Figured you'd like some coffee," Arvin said. "And we're having fettuccini, cod, and broccoli for dinner. Want to stick around?"

Robert smiled. "Oh, yeah. You know how to bribe a man. I'd kill for a beer, though."

"Tough luck. Rene's next batch won't be out for a week."

"I've heard. Anyway, sure, I'll talk to him if you think it'll help."

"You're the mayor."

Robert glared at him, then shook his head and sighed.

After dinner, he jumped back home. Going inside his rock was like going into an old library, minus most of the books. There were bits of wood stuck to every available surface, scraps that he had spent a small fortune buying from the other miners, traders and support people that came up here to make a living. Two dozen real paper books adorned a small shelf above his computer/comm station. They represented the profits from three months of laser-mining an iron rock two-thousand klicks downbelt from here. Those in the Cluster that didn't call him The Mayor called him The Librarian. Not that he'd ever let anyone touch his books. They could go download something free to read, if that's what they wanted. The smell and feel of a book, though, *that* you couldn't download.

He sat in the chair at the comm station and strapped in. "Rosie, call Eddy please."

"In work. Waiting. Waiting. Link request not acknowledged."

"Is his comm system down?"

"Eddy Schwarz's comm system is not responding to my interrogative. Your request is being blocked."

"Blocked?"

"His system is functioning correctly. All local queries are being blocked."

Robert sat back in his chair. Now that was odd. Maybe he should check in on the little prick. Eddy had quite a reputation for taking advantage of a situation, so there wasn't a man or woman in the Cluster who'd trust him enough to share air with him. He was a real bottom-feeder.

"Rosie, call RU12, please."

"In work. Waiting. Link established."

"Hello, Robert," a low voice rumbled out of the speaker.

"Hi, Rue."

"What can I do for you today, Mayor?"

"You have monitors floating all over in the Cluster, right?"

"Perhaps."

Robert sighed. When he was a kid, AI didn't exist, and robots didn't say things like "perhaps". They were just computers with legs. "I've been told that Eddy has a problem with waste venting out of his rock," he said. "Do you have recordings of that, and when it's been happening?"

RU12 held up a digit. "Hang on. Let me just access some records." It sat and stared at Robert for a moment. "Got it. What do you have for trade?"

That's my Rue, Robert thought. "You know I'm

doing this for the Cluster," he said, "not for me. This benefits everyone."

The robot rolled both orbs. "Well, then, what does everyone have for me?"

"Rue, you're such a friggin' mercenary. The leak is affecting you, too. You have a solar collector, don't you? Is the efficiency down?"

RU12 sat still for a moment, checking numbers. Finally, he nodded. "Very well. If you offer to clean my solar collector and eliminate the effusion, then I can give you the information you need."

Clean his collector. Great. "If you want, I'll be happy to clean your clock at the same time."

"Obscure cultural idiom noted. No, you need not 'clean my clock.'" RU12 nodded at Robert. "I'm sending you data for the last month. Effusion has been continuous, and has been gradually increasing in volume, as though the breach is expanding." An inset screen appeared next to RU12's head with the data.

"Damn. That much?"

"Perhaps Eddy is dead." The robot looked thoughtful, staring off-screen. "No, it appears that he took a jumpship upbelt ten days ago, most likely to the Ceres Cluster."

"After the leakage started."

"Apparently."

Robert considered asking RU12 if it could monitor Eddy's habitat control system, but even if it could, it wasn't likely to tell him so. More secrets. If he was going learn why Eddy had abandoned maintenance on his rock, then he'd have to go inside and have a look.

"Rue, can you erase our conversation?"

"Not to be concerned. It's highly encrypted."

"Not on this end."

"Yes, even on your end."

Robert's hair rose on the back of his neck. Bastard robot. "Okay, fine. Thanks for the information, and once this is cleared up, I'll see about getting your collector cleaned off."

"If you intend to enter Eddy's habitat, I would suggest enlisting the aid of Coella Wilson. She is intimately familiar with the mechanisms for Eddy's airlock, having repaired at least three of that type in the belt in the last four years."

"So you read minds, too."

RU12 barked an electronic laugh, reached out, and shut off the comm link.

Coella and Chin came in from her claim twenty hours after Robert contacted her. She met Robert on an uninhabited asteroid less than a klick from Eddy's. Around her waist was a belt crammed with tools. She was about a foot shorter than Robert, but he knew that she could beat the crap out of any miner in the Cluster, providing considerable entertainment to the locals while 'unwinding' at the Crystal Cup. Not that Robert thought she was unapproachable, you just had to understand that when she said she wanted to "take someone out," she usually didn't have dating in mind.

"How's your new claim going?"

"That little turd Chin is going to take half my profits with those damned nanites of his."

"So...you have the rock, but the nanites are doing all the work?"

She glared at him through her shaded visor, not an easy task. "Yeah, whatever. Still my claim." She pointed at Eddy's home. "Is that haze around his rock what I think it is?"

"Yeah, unfortunately. I don't know how we're going to get the suits clean after this."

"I'd say he owes us."

"I just hope he doesn't return while we're inside."

They both jumped to Eddy's home, coming to rest next to the airlock. The habitat's rocky surface glistened with a sheen of frozen slime, and the solar collector was darkened to near uselessness.

"Guess he wasn't expecting to move back in soon," Robert said.

"Let's crack this nut. If this goo keeps building up on our suits, I won't be able to see shit. Or, rather, that's all I'll be able to see." Coella opened her tool belt and made short work of the airlock mechanisms. They moved to either side of the airlock as it opened to avoid the inevitable blast of air, but the airlock was already evacuated. It was dark inside.

She pulled out a flashlight and shined it inside. "His entry light's burned out. Still has power, or the lock wouldn't have opened."

"I doubt the air inside is any good."

"Probably not. Here, make yourself useful." She

handed him the flashlight and got to work closing the outer lock and opening the inner. Fifteen minutes later, they stepped inside into darkness. Coella pulled out another flashlight, sweeping it over the inside of the habitat. Dead, rotting vegetation clung to every surface. She jumped, grabbing Robert's shoulder as a small cleaning bot zipped by her head, collected a piece of floating vegetation, and disappeared into a disposal cabinet.

"God Damn!"

"What?"

"Aw, it's nothin'"

"Coella, what is it?"

She looked away from him. "I downloaded the Aliens collection last month, and watched the whole thing. Never again, I swear."

Robert snorted.

"You think that's funny?"

"Aliens, right." He pushed a switch on the control panel to bring up the lights, hoping that the batteries still had enough of a charge on them. The lights flickered on hesitantly, strobing the room into clarity. Coella gasped.

There was clearly still air in the room, but neither of them bothered reaching for their helmet release clasps. A few tiny bits of green struggled in the mass of black rotting plants, and a host of fungi covered the walls.

Robert stared, and took a deep breath. "Are those portabellas?" he whispered. Huge, white, round bulbs of fungus stood out like molars in the decaying mass of plants.

She slowly scanned the room. "Did Eddy do this on purpose?"

"Dunno. Let's look around."

"No need. I can see why his recycler is dumping waste into space. It's probably jammed up solid with veggie-mass the cleaning robots have been feeding it, and the back-pressure blew out a seal. No wonder it's getting worse. It's not feces we're covered with, it's rotten plant scuz."

"Oddly, I feel a little better for that." He swept the flashlight over the dying mass of plants. "So the only mystery is why." Robert sat down at Eddy's monitor. "What do you want to bet that he doesn't use a password on his communications console?"

Coella smiled. "No bet. Nobody breaks into someone else's home."

"Uh-huh." He powered up the comm center and sat down at the computer. He wiggled his fat, suited fingers over the little keys of the keyboard. "This is going to be a bitch." He logged on, bypassed the password screen by hitting 'return', and found himself looking at Eddy's files. "Thanks, Eddy, for being such an obliging fellow."

It didn't take long to figure out that Eddy was getting a pricey habitat in the Ceres Group. MoleTech, one of the bigger and meaner corporations vying for control of most of the belt's assets, had made him a ridiculously high offer on his existing rock.

"MoleTech? They're the guys that bought out Jeremy's and Charl's rocks," Coella said. "What are they after?"

Robert tapped slowly against the plastic of his visor, thinking. "I don't think there's anything special about Eddy's rock. Before it was turned into a home rock, there was a pretty thorough assay done. Still...if MoleTech is interested, something's up."

"Call one of the guys that sold out and ask. One of them is bound to tell you something useful. You trust any of them?"

"Not really. What else would make MoleTech interested in our cluster?"

"Maybe something besides asteroids?"

Robert laughed.

"No, seriously," Coella continued, "if I remember right, when we joined the Cluster, we signed something that gave some percentage ownership to any patents we came up with."

A flashbulb illuminated the inside of Robert's head. "Ah," he muttered, "the lichen."

"Liking what?"

"No, I said lichen. It's that flakey gray stuff that's growing on some of the asteroids. A vacuum life form. A patented vacuum life form. The first."

Coella nodded slowly. "That would fit the bill. So how does buying up Eddy's asteroid give them control of the Cluster?"

"That's what I'm not sure about. Maybe I can just call Eddy at Ceres and tell him he's got a leak and milk him for information." He shut down the computer and switched off power to the comm station. "We should leave this place the way we found it."

"Like he's coming back. He owes us two clean suits. I'm at least taking those with us."

"Yeah, okay." Robert looked around at the fungi-covered walls. "And let's see if we can find a carrier bag. I'm taking the portabellas."

By the time Robert got back to his rock, he'd decided to call Frank Jones, one of the eleven founders of the Cluster. If anyone knew the ins and outs of Cluster legalities, Frank did.

Frank frowned at him through the comm screen. "So you're telling me Eddy sold out?"

"Yup. Jeremy and Charl, too."

Frank counted up on his fingers. "And Ralla and Earl and Joey. Son of a bitch, they'll have a majority with that weasel Eddy. Never could trust that lazy little prick."

Robert's breath whooshed out of his lungs. "That's...bad."

"Yeah, well, no shit. Last time MoleTech took over a colony, most everyone in it was dead by the time the takeover was complete. That was the Whiterock Cluster, you remember?"

"Yeah, I remember." Miners still occasionally came across bodies drifting in the belt from that event. He shuddered. "Are there any loopholes in the bylaws?"

"Let me send you a copy. You know any good lawyers?"

"In the asteroid belt?"

Frank laughed harshly. "Right. Never mind."

"Can't you guys just change the bylaws?"

Frank shrugged. "Sorry, changes need a two-thirds vote, and they can already block that. You find anything else in there, you give me a call and we'll work it, okay?"

"They might be after Sherrie's lichen patents, you know."

"Oh. Oh crap." Frank rubbed the coarse stubble of a two-day beard.

"What?"

"Nominally, the Cluster gets twenty-five percent of her profits. But if she dies and has no heirs, they get the whole shebang."

"And she has no heirs, I'm guessing."

"You hit the vein with the first blast."

"Great. Not likely she's getting married this week."

"Nope. She's married to her research already."

"Well, whatever MoleTech's motives, it doesn't bode well for the rest of us."

"No, it doesn't."

They broke communications and Robert carefully read the file that Frank had sent him. There weren't a lot of loopholes to jump into. Eleven owners, eleven rocks, one vote each, rules for transfer of ownership and thus voting rights. Some of the laws could essentially make corporate slaves out of anyone working in the Cluster, laws apparently never enforced or even mentioned by the original founders. The homesteads that had joined the Cluster could be treated as property of the Corporation. The founders probably never figured on the Cluster turning into a complete free-market community.

He sighed and drifted away from the screen.

Maintaining residence in Eddy's cesspool of a home would really be a trial for some poor front-man working for MoleTech, but not an insurmountable task. MoleTech could clean it up in a week, anyway.

There had to be a reasonable solution to this.

Vince Bloodwell, the CEO for MoleTech, sipped at his cappuccino and looked over the documents on-screen. "This is just a delaying tactic, isn't it?"

Penwick, the company's head lawyer, looked over his shoulder. "It's a lien against the asteroid for damages that the leakage caused. If we decided to fight it in court, it could take months. I suggest we pay the money for the cleanup and get on with satisfying the occupancy requirements. In three months, the Cluster will be ours to do with as we please."

"This does mean that they've figured out we're after the Cluster, and if they aren't idiots, they know why." He rolled his fingers on the oak desktop, glaring at the document. "This Robert Loaghrin, he's causing a bit of trouble for us."

Penwick smiled. "Once we own the Cluster, we can deal with him as we wish."

The best part of all, Robert thought, was that MoleTech was paying for this. Clean-up! One of the many accepted methods of cleaning dirty surfaces on solar arrays was to wipe them down or blow them off. Both of these techniques used up very precious materials, were labor intensive, and often had the same effect as using a leaf blower to blow leaves into your neighbor's yard. But if you weren't particular about damage to the surface you were cleaning, then heating up the contaminants to plasma temperatures worked very well, and assured that the contaminants would reach escape velocity from the Belt and thus not settle back down on someone else's equipment.

Without optical filters, Eddy's Rock looked like a fireball. They'd be able to see this from Earth. Better, the Ceres Cluster upbelt had to see it, too. Well, at least they would when the light arrived. They were over two light-minutes away. They'd likely figure it for one of the many ships zipping around the Belt; Robert had had the foresight to file a flight-plan for the Cluster's biggest ship to cover for this event, though the ship would never actually move from its port.

"Rue, can you tell if it's moving?" Robert broadcast.

"Oh, quite definitely. The plasma from Eddy's waste stream is hitting an easy 10K. Eddy's Rock is accelerating at about 0.1 gee. Between everyone's reflectors and mining lasers, you're pumping close to forty megawatts into the plasma cloud."

Getting everyone in the Belt to agree to redirect their solar thermal reflectors and lasers hadn't taken much arguing; they knew what was at stake. The individual directional controllers were all currently slaved to a master controller that RU12 had programmed to track Eddy's asteroid. Getting enough water to refill Eddy's storage tanks had been a task, but was fortunately part of the standard maintenance contract everyone signed when they joined the Cluster. Otherwise, Robert knew, there wouldn't have been enough reaction mass to do what he wanted to do.

Frank keyed in, "You can actually see it moving now."

Robert tweaked the filters on his viewer to dim the view. "Yeah. It's starting to rotate."

"The thrust vector of the leakage is not through the CG. We knew it would rotate," RU12 reminded him.

Robert nodded. RU12 was saying this for the sake of the other listeners in the Cluster. The rotation would get worse as the rock accelerated; fortunately the reaction mass spun away with the rotation, so the only real thrust-pulse the rock was getting was while the waste stream was pointed toward the rest of the Cluster.

"Twenty meters per second. Five RPM."

"Sweet." He grinned as Eddy's Rock slowly accelerated away from the Cluster. The reflectors and lasers provided a spotlight for the new star for nearly fifteen minutes before beam divergence made them useless. RU12 shut down the lasers and redirected the solar collectors/reflectors back to the mundane task of keeping people alive.

The cherry-red ember of Eddy's Rock faded into the stars.

The Crystal Cup was the only bar in the Cluster, and for that matter, the only one within 10,000 kilometers of the Cluster. It took substantial delta-vee (or time—your choice) to get to Carlton's Space Bar upbelt, and the clientele weren't nearly as friendly. The Cup hung at the end of multiple steel tethers, counterbalanced by another massive chunk of rock, orbiting each other just fast enough to keep the beer carbonated and in a glass. One of life's little pleasures, cherished by all the miners.

William Becher stood in the middle of the common room, incongruously lacking a beer, and shouted at Robert. "Where the hell is my asteroid?" Becher was large, ugly and imposing, and he could glare a hole in sheet steel, but Robert took his steady stare like he was basking in sunshine. Becher didn't have to tell them who his employer was; he may as well have had MOLETECH tattooed on his forehead. Two weeks after MoleTech had signed the agreement for the Cluster to start the clean-up, Becher had showed up to move in to Eddy's rock, establishing legal residency. Robert had set up this meeting at the Crystal Cup, since it was the only place big enough to hold this many people. And the new batch of beer was ready.

"Eddy's asteroid is no longer in the Cluster," he said.

"I can see that, asshole. What I want to know is where it is." Three other men stood with Becher, presumably the cleanup crew for Eddy's Rock. They didn't look like they were up for a fight, and glanced nervously at the crowd of miners bristling around them. Coella stood at the front of the crowd, just waiting for Becher to do something stupid.

Robert sipped at Rene's latest beer and smiled. He was completely astounded that the secret had lasted this long, considering that everyone living in the Cluster knew about it. "We're not entirely sure where it is. Some very hot gases exploded out of the side of it while we were cleaning off the surface and it accelerated out of the system last week. Really hot gas, just like a rocket. You should have seen it."

"A big rocket." Becher glanced around at his men. "You mean to tell us that that big-assed rocket that Ceres saw last week was Eddy's asteroid?"

Robert nodded again and took another sip. For some weird reason, this batch tasted better than any he'd had in a long, long time. They'd be lucky to find Eddy's asteroid and catch up to it in less than a year; it was covered with baked-in black carbon, making it optically nearly invisible, to say nothing of the fact that they'd boosted it into a hyperbolic orbit; it wouldn't be coming back. Sure, MoleTech could probably take the optical data from the "launch" and figure out where it went, but they'd still have to figure out how to inhabit an asteroid that was now spinning at 80 revolutions per minute. Catching it and slowing it back down would be prohibitively expensive. Of course, if Becher couldn't establish residency, MoleTech didn't get their precious vote.

Keeping them from doing this again would be difficult though; they still only needed to buy one more vote for a majority, and right now the votes were tied up. But that was for the future. Today, there was victory.

"And where the hell did you get a rocket that size?" Becher shouted. "There will be hell to pay when we find out who mounted it on our asteroid."

Hell to pay. Robert just smiled and lifted his pint.

"That might be," he said, "but in the meantime, cool your heels and have a beer. It's the best in the Cluster."

Author's Notes on "Wasted Space"

I like these characters. Personally, I think Robert has a thing for Coella. If you like these stories, let me know. I'll spend some time creating a few more in the same universe.

I'd like to write an asteroid mining story that uses the song "Big Bad John" as a plot foundation. But, that's another story.

Ashes to Ashes

The drive out to the foothills had been worth it. Below them, the city was covered with a blanket of white fog; above, the broad swath of the Milky Way painted the cold night sky. A bright orange streak suddenly bloomed into existence, then faded quickly. The two men lowered their binoculars.

"Did you see it?" Howard whispered.

Robert nodded. "That was really bright. Didn't hardly need the binoculars." He was loud and irreverent. All the crickets within hearing fell silent. "It's hard to imagine someone would pay five grand just to launch their ashes into orbit. I mean, they're dead, right?" Without waiting for an answer, he rambled on, "And it's just a bunch of dead body cells burned to ash once already. Not like they're sending their soul to heaven or something, or that they're going to enjoy the ride. And they don't even get to see it. Just doesn't make any sense." He paused to take a noisy sip from a steaming thermos cup. "So this guy was a friend of yours?"

"Yeah, very close." Howard spoke softly. "He planned ahead with his ashes. He started young, thinking about it. Saved fingernail clippings and hair. Added baby teeth to the lot. When he had his tonsils removed, he talked the doctor into letting him have them for an imaginary science project. That was before doctors started calling everything a biohazard. When he cut himself building a balsa model plane, he added a bit of blood to the lot. Even a tumor he had removed— he had to bribe a doctor to get that back—became part of the bounty that eventually became part of his ashes."

Robert made a retching sound. "Like a witch's brew," he said. "You're friend was nuts. I'll bet his heirs were pretty pissed off, him throwing away all that money on a space burial."

"Throwing away? It's the only chance he ever had to go to space. He dreamt of it ever since he was a child; walking on the moon, exploring Mars. But at his age— this was his only chance, as symbolic as it may be. Dreams became ashes." Howard gazed longingly at the distant stars. "He paid for a package deal with the burial company. For an extra twenty-five grand, he got a moon burial package and a deep space package. They don't send the whole body, you know. Most of it stays here on dear old Earth. They just send a few grams of ashes taken from the total."

"I'm surprised his descendants didn't call a lawyer.

What a freaking waste of money."

Howard laughed. "That's what he figured would happen, too. Once he was dead, his money-grubbing kids would cancel the whole show. But he planned for that."

"Yeah?"

"Like you said, it's just a bunch of dead cells from a body. It's nearly irrelevant that the host might still be alive. He arranged it so he could see it all, know that his intent had been executed and observe the bright pyre of reentry himself. He just burned to ash what he'd already gathered and called it part of the corpse to be. A premeditated partial death."

Robert gaped in disbelief. "And you knew—know—this guy?"

Howard sighed and shook his head. "It's me, you idiot. It's me."

Some author notes on "Ashes to Ashes"

Obviously flash fiction. I always felt it was sad that people don't get to see their own funeral, or what effect their lives have made on others. In fact, I started writing a book years ago called, "Things You Can Do When You're Dead," which was a little bit philosophy and a little bit a collection of weird stuff you could do that people might comment on years after you were dead. Like having a friend send pre-written letters to people you knew when you were alive.

Anyway, this story was kind of a spin-off from that book, which will probably never see the light of day. Some things are just too weird to write. Speaking of which, next up is a weird story called "Easy." You should read it, but I guess that's why you're here, isn't it?

Easy

The first time Joe heard the big red button telling him, "That was easy," he chuckled. Sure, it was an advertising gimmick for an office supply store, but the irony killed him.

He was at work, where they had just finished lifting a satellite onto the top of its booster, encapsulating it in its payload fairing, and arming most of the pyros and zip cords for the separation events after launch. Sweaty work, to say the least, amplified by the need for constrictive, confining clean-room suits that looked like high-tech blue burqas with rubber soles. So when a coworker slapped that big red toy button on her desk, and it said in its confident voice, "That was easy," Joe was very amused.

The button's casual assurance that every action in life was an easy stroll down an elm-bordered shady sidewalk, countered by the twisted and rocky path of reality, took a hold of his brain with the brute strength of an evangelically infectious meme. Inspired, Joe took it home.

That night, he placed the button on the floor, set up a video camera facing the button, and started recording. He put a tie-dyed sweatband on his head and did thirty pushups, smacking his forehead into the button, every time eliciting a "That was easy" echo of his forehead banging into it. Taken by the muse of idiocy, he sped up near the end for a Max Headroom earbuzzing articulation of "That that that that was *easy*!" It was as moronic as you can get, but when the video hit YouTube, it got over 50,000 hits. Who would sit through something like that?

More importantly, who would do something that stupid and film it? Joe would.

Joe needed fame like a programmer needed Jolt. Thus far it had been limited to the same venues that most attention-seekers found, with karaoke on the weekends at the local pub, pushing his blog like a cheap drug on unsuspecting friends, or being the donut guy on Friday. Just so long as someone would, for a moment, pretend that the monotony of his life had some meaning, some bearing on the motion of the universe. But, in fact, Joe's unquenched desire for a bit more than his allotted fifteen minutes of fame was an impending disaster waiting for the right tool with which to implement its destruction.

And Joe found that tool.

Joe discovered that there was a local half-marathon the next weekend only an hour drive from his apartment. He got the great idea to stand at the finish line, camera rolling, and hold out the button for the marathoners to whack as they came across the finish line. Twelve of the marathoners actually saw the button and slapped it on the way by, happily receiving their electronic "That was easy" after 13 miles of grueling pain. To Joe's delight, one of the marathoners laughed so hard that his wobbly legs collapsed under him, where he rolled on the ground and continued to laugh, despite his skinned kneecaps.

Joe got 80,000 hits from that video. Somehow Staples didn't jump on this free advertising bonanza, which is just as well for them. Sometimes "free" comes with a hefty handling charge.

Other events followed. Wherever someone was doing something truly extraordinary, Joe was there with his camera and the big red button. He managed to get an Olympic weightlifter to smack the button after winning the Gold. He was there when Jared Jenkins won the tightest race ever in California's gubernatorial election, happy to declare "That was easy" via the bright red button. He sent the button with Mark Satterfield when he made it to the top of Everest, and he faked a video of Neil Armstrong depressing the button after he arrived on the moon (conscientiously leaving out the sound, since it was "in a vacuum"). Ramsey Holstead, the famed brain-surgeon, did him the honor of tapping the button on his way out of the first-ever brain transplant between two consenting, but highly disturbed, adults.

These all got great responses on YouTube. But, as with all pop-cultural fads, this too, had to fade away into apathetic obscurity. The formulaic recounting of incredible feats followed by a button-tap only had so much carrying power. And Joe couldn't handle that. People had gotten tired of the joke.

Joe sulked. Joe fumed. He had over five hundred Facebook friends whom he'd never met who wouldn't talk to him. His blog readership had eight stalwart readers, and three of them were fake accounts he'd set up himself to pump up his ratings.

He would have happily sold his pathetic soul to regain the delectable fame he had tasted. But it was really an accident that put him on the dark and meandering path into depravity, leading to his subsequent rebirth into self-absorbed glory.

There are few more powerful visuals than a fireman stepping out of a disaster. Joe knew that. He'd watched the Towers fall. So Joe went to a burning house with his button and camera. And he didn't really mean for it to go bad at first, but the excitement and pressure of the situation dragged him ineluctably forward into his own personal swamp of emotional corruption.

Fireman Max Scheinfeld was carrying someone out of a burning house.

Joe got in his face and shouted over the wailing sirens and roar of fire hoses and fire, "Hit the button! Hit the button!"

Max jerked his head toward him and shouted back, "What the hell?"

"The button!" Joe's camera was set up twenty feet away, taking in the scene. He held the Easy button out for Max.

"Get the fuck out of the way!" Max pushed past Joe

and put the boy he was carrying down on the lawn on a blanket. He did quick checks on the boy and started in on CPR. Joe stood to the side, nervously reluctant to move into Max's reach and instead just watched him work on the boy. After two minutes, Max stood up and walked back toward Joe, his smoldering eyes and terrible grimace making Joe's knees shake.

But Joe, being Joe, gingerly held out the button, waiting for Max to do his duty. Max smacked the button out of Joe's hands, drove his face into Joe's, and screamed, "You fucking asshole!"

The boy on the grass lay unmoving and untended, like a broken doll.

Max turned away and went back to the task of putting out the fire before it worked its wrath on adjacent houses. Joe ran after His Precious, which to his relief had landed on the thick carpet of grass and came out unscathed from Max's angry blow. He grinned maniacally at his camera with a thumbs-up, and shut it off.

The YouTube video got just under a million hits. Joe was back in the game.

Joe was no fool. He figured it out. What he needed was some good old-fashioned Geraldo Rivera trash video, something to give his viewers whiplash as they turned away from the screen.

His next video presented a war vet, Jimmy Laredo, coming home from Iraq. Jimmy's legs and one arm were missing, his left eye covered with a patch. Fortunately, Joe thought, all he needs is one eye and one arm to hit my button. Joe was in the crowd as the war hero rolled down the ramp off the plane in his wheelchair. He held out the button hopefully before anyone knew he was there. The shocked and crowded mass of people became deathly quiet as they realized with disgust what was happening. Jimmy stopped and stared at the button, looking up in disbelief into Joe's anxious and expectant eyes. He covered his remaining eye with his remaining hand and began to cry.

Joe had twelve stitches and two broken ribs that he took home from that event. His camera was destroyed, but the SIM card survived. YouTube blessed him with well over ten million hits. Depraved humans worldwide rejoiced in Joe's unidirectional path to Hell. Joe had become an internet phenomenon, a cultural icon amongst the lowest forms of life inhabiting the digital pathways, a pariah for everyone else, but as with the videotaped lopping of heads, innocents could not help but be drawn into the decaying morass of his vision.

Once Joe healed up and purchased a new camera using the exceptional wealth acquired through tee-shirt and DVD sales, he dove into his next project. William Shandon had just finished a prolonged trial, not because of any question about his guilt, but because it took a long time to present the evidence from thirty brutally raped and vivisectioned young women. Jurors were replaced a number of times as they broke before the waves of horror crashing against their minds. Joe went to visit Shandon a week after he went to jail. He wanted to catch him before Shandon received the thirty death sentences that they handed down. A few bribes in the right hands from his newfound wealth let him bring in his worn Easy button and a video camera. He even got a guard to hold the camera for him.

Joe said, "You've admitted to murdering and essentially dissecting thirty women while they were awake."

Shandon smiled lazily, and rolled his eyes up in his shaved head, reliving the memories. "Oh, yeah, Yeah, I did, baby. There was this pregnant one…"

"Yeah, yeah," Joe interrupted, "I heard about that. So call it thirty-one. Can you do one thing for me, for my viewers? They want to know just what you thought about killing all those people." He held out his button like a golden chalice, hands shaking. Little beads of sweat broke out on his forehead, not from fear, but from tense excitement. This would be his crowning achievement, his pinnacle of fame, his virtuoso performance.

Shandon met his eyes and grinned, showing teeth like a rabid badger. He looked down at the big red button, reached out with both manacled hands, and stroked the blood-red surface. He closed his eyes, sighed and pressed it. The button squeaked and clicked, and the happy electronic voice declared to the world, "That was easy!"

From a starship thousands of kilometers above, the Watchers had been monitoring humans for over four thousand years. They were sentient single-celled amorphous blobs with crystalline minds, tennis-ball-sized with the ability to produce a variety of flagella-like appendages to help propel them around their liquid-filled ship. The Watchers had never been seen or detected by humans at all, despite the conviction of many humans that aliens were among them already. The Watchers, in fact, had never been on the surface of the planet, and possessed technology that assured that electromagnetic, gravitational, and neutrino detectors could in no way sense their presence. They were technically advanced millions of years beyond humans. Avoidance was trivial.

Most of the Watchers knew over a dozen human languages and had nearly perfect translators for those languages that they didn't speak. Not only could they detect and interpret the primitive electronic transmissions humans vomited forth every which-way into space, they could remotely monitor simple human speech from thousands of miles away using devices that human language is not yet fit to describe.

"This Joe fellow, K'othek commented, "is a real floater. He pollutes everything around him."

K'othek was referring to the impolite practice of excreting a ball of waste in the swimming fluids they all occupied.

C'tulu bobbed up and down. "True, true! And five hundred million followers! We should prepare for another Yucatan event!"

K'othek waved a dozen flagella in irritation. "Your solution is always to wipe out everything. You just like dropping asteroids."

"Not true!"

T'oktal, the youngest of them, blew gas into the fluids around him disdainfully. "You've dropped asteroids on three promising saurian civilizations on this planet. Before they even had any tech."

"Saurians are such unpleasant creatures."

T'oktal bobbed in agreement. "So true. But this Joe, his followers may be little more than momentary voyeurs, returning to normalcy when the nuisance is removed."

"Well."

"You still want to drop a rock."

He looked as sheepish as a tentacled tennis ball could look.

"I think," said T'oktal, "a more limited response is called for."

"Spontaneous combustion!"

T'oktal nodded. "That would suit. Humans never will figure out what causes it."

K'othek looked at the two of them. "Fine. But T'oktal does this job. I don't want C'tulu to get into the habit."

T'oktal tried to act calm, but inside his borvils had congealed in excitement. "If I must."

They swam over to what was euphemistically called the Fine Tuning Console and entered Joe's coordinates. The device would deliver a tightly collimated beam of microwave radiation to Joe's body as he lay quietly in bed. It would not ding when the cooking was done.

T'oktal flipped up the cover on the device and found himself looking at a big red button. He glanced at the others, but they appeared clueless. He sighed, and pushed the button.

He turned to K'othek, and opened his small mouth to say the words, then closed his mouth again without saying anything. There, he thought, lay the path to ruin, and he would not take it.

Some author notes on "Easy"

Easy was fun to write, but I wanted to make the main character as big an asshole as I possibly could, so the story became more disturbing and emotional than I expected, and then there's this huge shift to an almost Three Stooges alien scenario at the end. On the other hand, the outrageousness of the story allowed me to play with English more than I usually do.

I thought Joe was way over the top, but looking at the news today, I've discovered that there is no limit to assholiness. And if that isn't a real word, it should be.

Tom Jolly

Learning the Ropes

Mari Doromuala stared out the window of the top-floor office, down at the canals between the tall buildings, the tides and waves pushing the ocean water through the narrow channels. Dozens of small boats puttered in between, delivering goods, workers, supplies, and travelers like her. Here to make a proposal to a man with money.

It certainly wasn't the Miami of fifty years ago. Like the coasts of Choiseul, the island she came from, and her lost home in Poroporo, the streets were under a meter of water. You could still struggle from building to building through waist-high swells, or use one of the few high walkways spanning the submerged streets, but you didn't want to be outside in a storm. And you didn't want to be in this water anyway. It smelled of sewage. Thank God the building's air conditioner still functioned.

She turned away from the window when Bill Warner,

one of the team that ran engineering at Colonial Mars, Inc., entered the room. He held out his hand to her and said, "Mrs. Doromuala? I'm pleased to meet you. Please, have a seat." He motioned to an office chair next to a square table. The office was sparsely furnished, and the walls adorned with a variety of construction pictures from the Martian colonies. "I understand you have a proposal for us. You know we could have provided you with a variety of media aids to support your presentation, right?"

She saw the look in his eyes. If he'd done some background checks, he'd already know that she came from the Solomon Islands and would have made many assumptions about her education and abilities. "Mr. Warner, yes, I'm well aware of that." Mari was soft spoken and her accent was light, just enough to sound exotic without being difficult to understand. "But I did not want to put this proposal anywhere where it could be hacked." She placed a thin folder on the table in front of her and slid it over to him. He looked a little irritated at the suggestion that their computer system may not be secure, but didn't say anything. Few systems were truly secure anymore.

He stared at the closed folder for a moment then looked into her dark eyes. "Just so you're aware, I'm the first line of defense against quack proposals. If this gets by me, then you can present it in front of the owners, and they will decide if it has any merit. But if it's a load of crap, I'll know it. You understand? And a little salesmanship and bling isn't a bad thing."

She smiled at his frank admission. "I believe the

proposal will stand on its own legs," she replied.

Warner hunched his shoulders and flipped open the folder, reading the first of three pages, intermittently glancing up at Mari. By the end of page one, he started chuckling, picked up the pages, and leaned back in his chair. "Ten kilometers of carbon nanotube composite ribbon! Dear God," he muttered, shaking his head, but he was still smiling. Mari felt the tension in the air evaporate, but she knew he hadn't reached the end yet.

When he did, he frowned. "You want to head this mission?"

Mari nodded. "I've got the astronautical engineering degree. I've had pilot experience in the compact fusion runabouts, and over fifty hours EVA. I'd be perfect for the job."

Warner rubbed his chin. "The Solar Resources Commission will put you away when they figure this out. What of your family?"

"My family is dead, Mr. Warner. My home village, my husband and children, were all washed away during a tidal surge." She looked away from Warner, staring out the window, her thoughts far away. "Our home was already on stilts from the rising waters. The village was like a Venice made out of sticks. I was away at college when it happened, hoping to have a career and to make enough money to move them off what was left of Choiseul." She turned back and stared at him, her eyes filled with guilt and regret. "I did not finish in time."

Bill Warner sighed and closed the folder. "Sorry to hear that." He was silent for a few moments, then continued, "I suppose you're aware that the Solar Resources Commission has all the asteroid belt commerce tied up, right? All the miners sell ore through them, and they step on anyone that tries to get a foot in the door."

Mari nodded. "The SRC is a known monopoly," she replied.

"And they own most of the structures on Mars, leasing to anyone that needs a presence there. Not exactly conducive to colonizing the planet; it's hard for an entrepreneur to make a profit when half their income goes to rent. Likewise, the SRC has no interest in terraforming it long term or short term. They're interplanetary slumlords, you might say. The easier it is to run around on the surface, the easier it will become to colonize, and their rental monopoly would collapse."

Mari nodded again. "The project can be presented so that it appears to help them at little cost to them. I do not believe that they will interfere."

"We'll see," Warner said, drumming his fingers on the folder, watching Mari carefully. "So why is it that you want to go? What's driving you?"

"I live on a planet that is warming up rapidly, Mr. Warner. I do not know what will happen here, but I know that most of the people living here just do not care enough to stop it. They will cook like frogs in boiling water, given the chance. If I start another family, I want to start it on a planet where everyone cares. Where everyone understands what their actions mean, where they are all striving for a common goal, not bickering over the nature of reality." She shook her head angrily.

"My next home will be on Mars."

"If the SRC doesn't stop you."

She lifted her chin up, challengingly.

Bill Warner smiled slowly. "We'll get you that presentation with the owners of Colonial Mars, anyway. That's the first step. Then we'll have to see what sort of monkey wrench SRC throws in the gears."

Nearly a year later, Mari Doromuala had a ship named the Anteater. The name of the monkey wrench from the Solar Resources Commission was Alan Vickers. He showed up on the Anteater when Mari was going through the ship's manifest a month before launch date. She was expecting someone from the SRC since the ship was being leased from them, just not a grinning idiot with freckles and red hair.

The Anteater was only twenty-three meters long, with the last five meters reserved for the compact fusion reactor engines and another three meters for fuel tanks. The Anteater sat on the tarmac at the Mohave Air and Space Port like any other airplane, with the exception that it could get to orbit with a half-tank of fuel. Once it refueled in orbit, it could get to almost any rock in the solar system and back.

After Alan introduced himself as the "SRC Observer", Mari pointed out that if he wasn't coming along, she could have packed an extra hundred kilograms of ice cream.

"Or popcorn," he replied, deadpan. Mari almost smiled, but managed to refrain. Alan shrugged

Tom Jolly

apologetically. He followed Mari around the ship like a puppy dog, asking about everything the ship was carrying. Mari was ready for that.

"So this is the ten kilometer cable, huh?" They were standing next to a reel of twelve by three millimeter tape, two meters tall. "Smaller than I expected."

Mari nodded. "The tape is only 1600 kilograms. But it can handle two million Newtons tension."

Alan raised thick red eyebrows. "Wow. Tell me about the experiment. I read up on it, but some of it didn't make a lot of sense to me."

Mari frowned. Alan wasn't already suspicious, was he? Their cover story was pretty solid. "We'll be running tests on the cable to see if there are energy-generating capabilities by spinning it through the plasma of the solar wind. If it works, if the cable carries a current, then we might have a good new power source for the asteroid belt. Your SRC thinks they can make a lot of money from it, when CMI licenses it to them."

Alan looked blankly at Mari. They both new that SRC would just replicate the technology instead of licensing it from CMI once they had the data in hand.

"Impressive," he said, "but why attach the cable ends to two asteroids? Why not just spin the cable through the solar wind?"

"Multiple reasons, though some of them may not pan out experimentally. The primary reason is that if a current is produced, there will be associated counter force imposed on the spinning tether to slow it down. If we're using the rotation to produce energy, the larger the two

112

asteroids are, the longer the energy production will last. We'll pick two asteroids in the million-kilogram range with a relative velocity of around a hundred meters-per-second, half of which will become the circumferential velocity when they are finally tethered together. Naturally, we'll have to choreograph our movements to be in the right place at the right time to connect them together since the tether is only ten kilometers long. There may also be electrical effects due to the level of tension on the cable, but that's partly what the experiment is for."

"All well and good," Alan said, "but you're rotating a cable through a neutral plasma. Why do you expect to generate anything?" As he talked, Alan examined one of the remote-operations robots in its rack. The robots would do most of the dangerous work of drilling, installing the penetration rods and lift rings, and attaching the tether. They could just sit back and watch the operation if the robot's AI was good enough. Tethering a moving asteroid was a common practice; asteroid miners did it all the time to provide long-term artificial gravity on their own ships.

"The solar wind also contains sheets of magnetic waves, the heliospheric current sheet. We may also generate energy from that, just as early tether experiments generated energy by dragging a conductive tether through the Earth's magnetic field. There are several variations on the experiment we wish to test, also; if different metallic compositions of the paired asteroids contribute to the current generation, or if additional static fields or magnetic fields can vary the proton/electron balance enough to create a current flow in the tether, and so on. You've seen the list of planned experiments, right?"

"Yes, I have. I just wasn't sure what it all meant. Which is why I asked. You also have a remote thruster on the manifest, right?"

She smiled and nodded. "Some of the asteroids will have a little spin that we'll have to change, otherwise they'll try to roll up the tether like a yo-yo or oscillate at the end of the tether. We'll send out the stand-alone thruster and its programming will do the rest. Finding the right pairs of asteroids won't be an easy task; minimal spin, closing trajectories within ten klicks at less than a hundred meters per second, total mass under two million kilograms, maybe smaller asteroids with higher relative speeds, and both metallic."

"Why metallic?" Alan asked.

"Carbonaceous asteroids are more likely to come apart when they start spinning around on the end of the tether. And the attachment ring we install on the asteroid has to be implanted on the asteroid securely and deeply to handle the force we'll be putting on it. We can't use asteroids with a lot of ice, or gravel pits."

"Hmm. You expect this will take three months, huh?" He stared around the cargo hold at the variety of devices stashed and tied down in their holds.

Mari heard the underlying message; he would be bored to death watching her record data for three months, as she would use robots to do most of the extra-vehicular work. That was good; bored meant inattentive. He wouldn't notice some of the things she had to do to make this work.

Over the next two weeks, Mari taught Alan to play Go on the ship's table computer, starting him off with a nine-stone handicap. He became immersed in the game, which meant she had to answer fewer pointed questions. Distracting him, after all, was the main goal of the game, but she also learned a lot about him from how he played. There were no spontaneous moves—each move he took was deeply considered, the same way he performed every task he did on the ship.

The first game they played took nearly a day, interrupted continuously by the simple but constant regimented tasks that were required when living in a spaceship. After two weeks, Alan could come close to a tie with only a three-stone handicap. Losing didn't seem to bother him, either, and he never lost his temper. A bad mistake provoked nothing more than tight lips and a nod, acknowledging a cheap lesson in tactics. If he wasn't the enemy, she thought, she might actually begin to like him.

Once they arrived in the asteroid belt, it took them over a week to find the first pair of acceptable asteroids. They had nearly two days to prep the two before they came within range of each other. Robot workers drilled down into both asteroids and secured the two attachment rings and oscillation damping system. Mari had explained to Alan how important the center of gravity was on the asteroid; any offset and the asteroid would wobble back and forth on the end of the tether as the pair rotated, inducing a varying tension based on the wobble frequency.

After a day of data sampling, the cable was released. Alan had been concerned with the snap-back of the cable under tension, but part of the chemistry of the cable included cross-linked connections between adjacent nanotubes that converted the tension release into heat. The cable appeared to shrink rapidly when it was disconnected from both asteroids, pivoting around its center as it swung in a great circle. The disconnected asteroids tumbled on their ways at nearly the same relative velocity with which they began the experiment.

"How do we know they're on the same trajectories as before?"

Mari tried not to laugh at the question, but Alan could see she was amused by it, and he blushed. "They aren't," she said. "We've interrupted both their paths by tying them together for a day. They both have new trajectories." She shrugged. "It doesn't really matter, though, because they weren't known trajectories to begin with."

"But what if they're headed towards Earth now?"

"What if they were headed toward Earth before we started, and we just prevented the accident? We might be heroes! Besides, neither of these is large enough to make it through Earth's atmosphere." Probably, she thought. Not that it really mattered. She knew where they were going.

"No need to be sarcastic. You already know I don't care for this job that much. I mean, my job in general. This particular job isn't horrible. You're okay."

"High praise, indeed," she said, grinning.

"Except for the sarcasm," he sighed.

A month in, and they'd located, tethered, and tested a dozen pairs of asteroids with mixed results, mostly discouraging. An asteroid screening program monitored the trajectory of every asteroid within a quarter-million kilometers, usually a hundred or less at any given time, selecting pairs of small asteroids within the narrow criteria it had been given.

They were naming the asteroids as they released each pair, duly recording the orbital parameters of each one as it flew off. This pair was Abbott and Costello. One was twice as large as the other. Ben and Jerry were next up on the list. The disconnected tether spun slowly in space until remote units put the end clamps under light tension and slowed it down using small thrusters.

Mari was pleased with how useful Alan actually turned out to be. Perhaps to avoid the boredom, or perhaps because he just enjoyed working with her, he insisted on doing most of the EVA work when it was needed, having a strong background as a vacuum maintenance tech. Expecting constant tension between them, like two tethered asteroids, she found herself oddly relaxed around him, a slow orbit, despite the secrets she was withholding from him.

Alan was suited up and drifting just outside the cargo hold monitoring the tether respooling operation when an alarm went off. He immediately damped the alarm and shouted into his mike, "Mari, what the hell is going on?"

She didn't answer. He bit his lip and glanced quickly

around. Overhead, a trail of ice crystals jetted out of the top of the ship. Below, another smaller jet of ice sprayed from the ship. Entry wound, exit wound, Alan immediately thought. He hadn't bothered to tell Mari what his job was before he became an Observer, or what an Observer was expected to do when SRC regulations were broken. He spun quickly to the cargo bay airlock and said "Authority AV12789. Override safety switch and pressure interlocks. Evacuate cargo bay airlock."

The light on the door changed from red to green after an interminable five-second wait. He slapped the button to open it, stepped inside, and stared through the tiny window into the ship. He could see Mari at the control panel, limp and unconscious. There was a red streak across her forehead. "God dammit," he said, slamming his hand against the inner door.

"Please repeat request," the ship said.

"Close airlock outer door. Equalize pressure of airlock to interior pressure, then open inner door." He could hear the air rushing into the airlock over the sound of his own hoarse breathing while he stared anxiously at Mari.

It took another five seconds while he sweated. It wouldn't take long to drop to a hard vacuum inside the ship; when there was a breach, the ship locked in its existing air supplies. It didn't try to keep the pressure up while its precious resources drained to vacuum.

The hatch finally popped open and he slid it to the side. He grabbed the door frame, hurled himself to where Mari lay, and unbuckled her limp form. Above and below, he could see a gray cloud of condensing vapor as it crowded into the punctures in the ship's skin. There was deep gouge in her seat from the passage of the micrometeorite that holed the ship. He hoped that it was only secondary debris that had wounded her head, but the object had come too close to her to be certain.

He lifted her weightless form and lunged toward the airlock, trying not to look too closely at her head wound. Beads of blood floated in the air like red pearls.

The two of them crammed narrowly into the airlock. It was only built for one person. "Close the inner door," he said. "Repressurize."

The door slid shut and he heard the rush of air again. He finally relaxed as the hissing died down and the pressure light went to green.

"Anteater, redirect the remotes to retrieve the patch kits. Plug the two holes. Give me a diagnostic for any current damage to the ship when the holes are repaired."

"Confirmed," the ship replied. "Hole repairs are in work. Diagnostic test initiated."

He unfastened his helmet and Velcroed it to a wall, then finally looked at the gash in Mari's head, wiping away the blood with his thumb. It was just a shallow cut. He could see that she was still breathing and gave a sigh of relief. Trying to do CPR inside the cramped airlock would have been close to impossible.

She mumbled something and put her hand on top of his gloved hand. Their limbs were tangled in the tight quarters. She cracked her eyes open after a few seconds and frowned at him, reaching for his own face and wiping a tear away from his cheek.

"What's this?" Mari croaked weakly. "I'm the one that's injured, not you."

"You're okay," he said, voice quavering. "You're okay."

Every asteroid mining ship in the belt was equipped with a sensor array and dedicated computer that spotted and calculated the orbital parameters of every rock larger than five meters that came within its range. The parameters were sent to a central database that compared the data to known asteroids, eliminated duplications, and added whatever was actually new. Then, the central computer checked for the probability of a future collision with any celestial body that happened to be hosting humans.

When the first million-kilogram asteroid was discovered, destined to impact the Martian Isidis Planitia Basin at nearly eighteen kilometers per second, the Space Regulatory Commission deemed it a fluke, and thanked whatever Martian gods there were that it was going to miss the colonies near the Mariner Valley and the Tharsis region. It wouldn't hit for another three months, so there was plenty of time to warn away Martian research teams from the target area. There were suspicious members on the Commission, of course; Colonial Mars, Inc., had been begging for permission to drop asteroids on Mars for years. It seemed too convenient.

It wouldn't be a serious enough impact to make a significant difference in the climate; one nuke-sized explosion's contribution to the atmospheric density and thermal background certainly wasn't enough to provide t-shirt weather for the masses.

When a second similarly-sized meteor was discovered a week later, aimed at nearly the same place, the SRC knew something was seriously wrong and started looking for someone to hang.

Carolyn Abernathy, SRC's CEO, paced in her office and ranted at her lead scientist, Raf Burgess. "We're tracking all the asteroids! How did we miss this? And who is responsible?"

Raf made a calming motion with his hands, which seemed to infuriate her even more. "These asteroids are only five to ten meters wide. We aren't tracking all the asteroids, just the ones that are over fifty meters wide. We're only starting to build the database on the small stuff. There are literally billions of them."

"So we can't see these coming at all?"

"Not easily. We just don't have the resolution or assets," Raf replied.

"But can we chase them down and push them out of the way?"

Raf shook his head solemnly. "Nope. Too big a velocity change, too much fuel. Ships can't catch them if they aren't already headed that way."

"But someone is specifically aiming at Mars?"

Raf cleared his throat nervously and said, "It still could be a coincidence. Asteroids hit Mars all the time."

Carolyn glared daggers at him. "You've backtracked the trajectories, I suppose?"

"We have a general idea where they are coming from, yes. But million-kilogram asteroids take a lot of thrust to move around much; either a lot at once, or a little for a long time. We'd be able to see the thermal signature of the rocket. So far, all we've seen is the usual thruster signature from the miner runabouts. We can get an infrared telescope in place in about a week that'd be close enough to see any new incoming asteroids."

Carolyn chewed on her knuckles, her manicured nails carefully folded into her palm, and stared at a wide wall map of the asteroid belt. Owned assets were marked with hundreds of red pins. It looked like the map was diseased. "Get me a list of all the ships within a million klicks of the backtrack trajectory, all the way back up to the Belt. With their manifests. If it isn't a registered miner, then find out what the hell they're doing out there."

Her cell phone buzzed and she picked it up off her desk, glancing at the display. "Yes, Robert?" She listened for a moment, her face getting redder with each word, her teeth grinding like a gristmill. "Thank you, Robert," she said tersely, and disconnected, skewering Raf with her eyes. "That was number three. Aimed for the same damned region. Still think it's a coincidence?"

Raf looked over at the door to her office, thinking how nice it would be to be on the other side of it. "I'll get you that list," he muttered.

Mari received the stand-down order while Alan was still asleep. It wasn't like she had much choice; the ship was also outfitted with a remote engine cutout controlled by the SRC as a supposed "anti-piracy" function. She couldn't go anywhere even if she wanted to. The engines could still autonomously respond to an anti-collision effort, but otherwise, they weren't going anywhere except along their current trajectory. They'd be boarded within a few days, and that would be that. She'd be arrested and her duplicity with Alan Vickers would be revealed. When he awoke, he would read his own message from the SRC and he would suspect. He would ask a few questions, and then he would know.

She sighed heavily and went to look in on the snoring Alan, floating innocently ignorant in his bedbag. She considered her options. With his arms in the bag as they were now, she could tape him inside before he could open it up. Hold him captive, threaten to toss him out the airlock if she wasn't given a million dollars and a helicopter. Where would that get her? The engines still wouldn't work, and she'd actually come to like Alan a lot, even if he was "the enemy".

"Alan," she whispered in his ear. "Wake up." She gently shook him. He started suddenly, saw her there, and yawned.

"God, is it time to get up already? Do we have another test to run?"

"No. We have to talk." She looked over at the control panel. "Our engines have been shut down remotely by the SRC."

He rubbed his eyes groggily and dragged himself out of the bag. "Why would they do that? Did they message us?"

"Yeah, they did," she said. "They said they would be boarding us within fifty hours."

He stretched and craned his head to look at the computer screen. "What? Did they say why?"

Mari shrugged sheepishly. "No."

Alan dragged his fingers through his thickening red beard. "Weird. I'll message them and ask. Any guesses?"

She looked away from him, watching the digital viewports as though they would offer some escape from what she was about to tell him. "They might think we're lobbing asteroids at Mars to help terraform it."

His first instinct was to laugh at the ridiculous joke, and he slowly choked on it as he watched her stern face, straight posture, and folded hands. She was completely serious.

"We've been bombing Mars?" he asked incredulously.

She waggled her hand. "Kind of. You know when we do the tether tests and connect two asteroids together?"

"Uh-huh?"

"It's a ruse to do a momentum transfer between the asteroids. It puts one of the two asteroids on a collision course with Mars. Since we aren't using rockets, the change in orbit isn't visible or detectable."

Alan shook his head. "I know better than that, please. There's no way in hell you could get that sort of accuracy from a tether momentum transfer."

"You remember the standalone rocket we brought?"

Alan's face started to darken. "Yeah...?"

"It wasn't just to despin the rocks. It has a special

program to chase the target asteroid after release and fine-tune the orbital parameters as required. Give it a little nudge when needed. It comes back when the asteroid is on target, plus or minus a thousand kilometers at the impact zone."

He stared off at the wall, thinking and frowning, trying to work it all out in his head. "But…the velocity change needed to get to Mars from the belt is over two kips. You can't get that kind of orbital change out of a 100 meter-per-second delta-vee between the two asteroids. No way."

She shook her head. "We weren't using belt asteroids. We were using Mars-crossing asteroids. It didn't take much of a tweak. But the Anteater burned a lot of fuel maintaining our position at top of the ellipse."

Alan glared at her and rubbed his forehead. "You did all this right in front of me?"

"Hey, it wasn't easy. You're a smart guy."

Alan didn't look mollified. He gazed out the digital viewport and asked, "How many? How many times have we done this stupid fake tether test?"

"The test was real. The data is good," she said.

"Regardless, it wasn't really the object, was it?"

She shrugged. "We've located thirty-three pairs of close-velocity Mars-crossing asteroids with a similar inclination," Mari said. She was proud of the fact, talking loudly.

"Dear God. Thirty-three? How…how big are the impacts?"

"Average? Like, a Nagasaki each."

Alan winced at the flippant reference. "In Joules?"

"Fifty to a hundred terajoules. More or less."

"Each," he added.

She nodded.

Alan shook his head in disbelief and rubbed his face. "Why all the hocus-pocus with the tether? Why not just push the asteroids with the ship?"

"Do the math. A million kilogram asteroid with a velocity correction of a hundred meters per second? You remember the Falcon Heavy?"

"Well, yeah, of course."

"For that kind of delta-vee, I'd need that rocket strapped to the asteroid, firing for a full fifteen seconds. You think anyone might notice that?" she said.

Alan nodded slowly. "I see your point."

"And we get to reuse the tether with almost no refueling. Well, except for the fuel needed to move our ship to the next viable pair."

Mari watched him carefully as he clenched his teeth and glared at her. "This is like your Go game, isn't it? You distract me with moves that have nothing to do with your real intent, but the little distractions add up and create their own strength, right? All the information was there, but I couldn't see the overall plan for all the side-actions leading up to it."

She shook her head. "The game itself was the distraction. You can read any number of stories into the play of the stones. Sometimes sacrifices are made to achieve a goal. Sometimes pieces are played just to see how the other player will react."

He looked at her for a while longer. "I need to think," he said. "And pee."

Ten minutes later, Alan and Mari were sitting across from each other. Alan's anger seemed to have disappeared, replaced with concern.

"When the SRC finds out what you've done, they're going to arrest you," Alan said.

"Is dropping rocks on Mars actually illegal?"

He shook his head. "Not for that. For lying about what you were going to be doing out here. There are laws about that, and the SRC wrote most of them. SRC regulates most of the commerce in the asteroid belt. There are also the free miners, but the SRC is the only market they can sell to, so they tend to obey whatever laws and pricing the SRC imposes on them. As far as dropping rocks on Mars, that's under the purview of Colonial Mars, though the SRC owns most of the structures on Mars and it's not in their financial interest to see Mars terraformed. You said you were working with Colonial Mars, right?"

"That's correct."

"So they offered you up as the sacrificial goat?"

She smiled. "No. I have a plan. I just need to know if you will agree to it."

He leaned back and studied her. Mari felt her heart beating faster. *We have both changed so much in three months*, she thought. *Have we changed enough?*

"What sort of plan?" Alan asked.

"Before the SRC arrives, I can leave you outside with

a beacon and they pick you up. The Anteater and I will disappear."

"You have no functional engines," he pointed out.

She smiled enigmatically and shrugged with one shoulder. She'd smuggled some drugs onto the ship that would be easy enough to add to his food, and the drugs would knock him out long enough that he'd never see the how she left, if it came to that. Still, he might figure it out. He'd seen what the tether could do.

He leaned forward and took both her hands in his. He took a deep breath and let it out slowly. "I would...I think I would rather go with you, wherever it is you might be disappearing to."

Her dark eyes twinkled with delight, and she drew him into a hug, holding him tightly against her. He breathed in the scent of her hair against his face and sighed. After a minute, Alan pushed her away gently and said, "But how are you..." He was stopped with the soft pressure of her lips against his. He closed his eyes. Questions would wait.

"What do you mean the Anteater isn't here?" Captain Argus shouted at his crew.

Engineer Goldman stared at his display. "Their transponder started dopplering a few hours ago, and their vector seems to have changed by almost one kilometer per second, from the looks of it." He rubbed the stubble of his short hair nervously and glanced over at another screen. "We can pursue, but it'll add a couple more days."

"But their damned engines are disabled!"

Goldman nodded. "Yessir. But they still had their tether. SRC headquarters said they suspect the Anteater was using the tether for momentum transfer between asteroids to drop them on Mars without using any fuel. My best guess is that they latched the Anteater onto a big asteroid with their tether and used their own ship as one end of the bolo, reeling in the tether to increase their own velocity."

"What of the boy we had on board the Anteater? The Observer? Alan what's-his-name?"

Goldman shook his head. "No word from Alan Vickers, sir. There's been no communication with their ship since their engines were disabled. Headquarters thinks he could be dead, that this—Mari Doru—Dormu—whatever the hell her name is, took him out." He looked up at his Captain and said, "She comes from some headhunter tribe on some island, I've heard."

Captain Argus frowned at Engineer Goldman. "Keep your opinions to yourself, Goldman. And put us on an intercept."

"They could do this again, you know, if they come across the right asteroid."

The Captain grumbled, "Well then, let's hope they run out of food before we do. I hate the taste of Engineers."

The Anteater rattled like a 1920's jalopy, secured and hidden on the side of a megaton asteroid as it pounded through the thin edge of the Martian atmosphere. The deceleration would put both them and the asteroid in a highly elliptical orbit around Mars. Eventually, after a couple more atmospheric passes, the asteroid, named "Vasquez," would succumb to the pressures of Mar's tenuous breath and plunge into the surface, following the intent, if not the exact path, of its previous brothers and sisters.

Before that final descent, the Anteater would perform one more tether maneuver with Vasquez, borrowing a bit of its momentum with the help of a few nudges from their small remote thruster, putting them in a sufficiently high stable elliptical orbit. The remote thruster, a product of Colonial Mars, was still under their control, unlike the Anteater's silent main engines, and flitted around the ship like a bumblebee with its rear end on fire, gently pushing wherever needed.

The last maneuver they'd made in the asteroid belt used the tether to launch a much smaller asteroid out of the asteroid belt with the ship's transponder secured to its side. At least the errant asteroid bought them time. But Mari couldn't plan for everything that happened.

What she did plan for was an extra four months of food, with a bit to spare. Mars had always been her final target. What she hadn't planned for was an extra mouth to feed.

Twenty hours after leaving the safety of the asteroid, gaunt and weak, but happy, Alan and Mari sat together and watched Mars as they approached the low point in their orbit. Mari sent a tight-beam encrypted laser communication to let the Colonial Mars crew know they were there and sat back to wait.

The response only took minutes. Bill Warner's face appeared on their screen, hair tangled and bleary-eyed, as though he had just woken. He rubbed his hand on his face. "Mari! You're alive!"

"Bill Warner? I didn't expect to see you on Mars," Mari replied.

"I wanted to be on the welcoming committee." Bill looked off to the side. "Claudia, is this link secure? Good." He looked back at Mari and Alan, grinning. "I see you picked up a hitchhiker."

"Hello, Mr. Warner," Alan said, "I'm Alan Vickers. I believe I'll be looking for a new source of employment, if you can think of anything."

"There's no lack of work on Mars if you have a good brain," Bill said. "We'll get you set up with something. How about you, Mari? I understand you sent thirty-some gifts our way. They made quite a splash. Thanks to you, we have a boiling mud lake in Isidis now, except you can't see it for the all the steam."

Mari nodded. "Not really enough to do a lot of good, I think. A thermal drop-in-the-bucket."

"Yeah, well, about that. You were kind of the test case. We now have an open, public contract for any asteroid miner to drop rocks our way, paid by the megajoule, so long as they target the muddy puddle that Isidis Planetia has turned into. No payment if they miss! It's a hell of a deal for the free miners; they don't have to mine the rock at all, or process the ore, or deal with the SRC to sell their ore."

Mari looked doubtful. "But they don't have tethers."

Bill laughed. "Shortly after you shipped out, we sent up fifty tether sets supposedly destined for the Ceres elevator project. They, um, 'got lost' on the way there. Space pirates, no doubt. Since there's little thermal signature from using them, it's gonna be damned hard for the SRC to find the tethers without boarding every miner's ship in the belt, and rumor has it that some of the tether sets are being stored as free-floating objects. Unless someone has access to their orbital parameters, they're not likely to find them at all. My best guess is we have over a hundred small asteroids headed our way right now, and as their Martian bank accounts swell, more miners will get involved."

"But how can you pay…" she started.

He grinned wider and interrupted her. "Martian real estate has spiked recently, for those few in-the-know, and we've claimed a hell of a lot of it. Eventually, when SRC finally gets a clue, they'll get in on the gold rush and start claiming prime bits themselves. I expect that their structure rentals will be less profitable than their real-estate holdings in fairly short order, and then they'll take advantage of all the prep work we've done for them. God, you two look hungry. Are you okay?"

Alan and Mari looked at each other and smiled weakly. "We'll make it another day. Just send someone to get us."

Bill nodded. "That'll cost you, you know. It's $100,000 Martian dollars for a rescue, and then we'll have to let the SRC take their ship back."

"What? Are you serious?" Mari stuttered, her face

turning red.

"Yeah, really sorry about that. Anyway, we subtract that from the $3,000,000 you get for the asteroid deliveries, give or take a bit, and that only leaves you with a paltry $2.9 mil. Apparently there's a small bounty for the few Earth-crossing asteroids you took out of the equation, too. That'll have to be added in. It's enough for a comfortably equipped family berth in one of the Pavonis lava tubes. And maybe a few thousand acres on the outside, if you're planning for the long future."

Mari shook her head, a slow grin creeping back to her face. "Bill, you're really a bit of an ass."

He returned her smile and tilted his head to her. "I've been told that a number of times."

Mari laughed, reached out, and took Alan's trembling hand, squeezing it.

Tomorrow, they would be home.

Some author notes on "Learning the Ropes"

This is another story that required a decent amount of math, and some speculation about asteroid field density. I even checked the limits of material strengths for the cables used, then calculated how big the reel would be to hold it. The problems of doing what I proposed in the story are much bigger than I described; two non-spinning asteroids, once attached by a cable, would really wreak havoc when the cable started turning, the asteroids trying to climb up the cable like a yo-yo. Damping that effect would take a lot of energy or some sort of rotating axis attached through the CG of each asteroid. Believe it or not, I tried to simplify the explanation.

I found that with cable material strength limits, I couldn't get a high enough velocity change to take a belt-asteroid from the belt to Mars, so I had to depend on Mars-orbit-crossing asteroids. I mentioned that in the story. Fortunately, there are a lot of those, and it's fairly safe to say there are a hundred times as many in the size range I picked than there are of known asteroids. Probably a lot more.

Is dropping asteroids on Mars a viable terraforming trick? Anyone's guess. It might toss so much debris into the atmosphere that it cools the planet further. It might put up so much water vapor that it traps even more heat from the Sun. The impact itself would sure as heck add more heat, just from the kinetic energy involved.

The cool idea in the story, from my viewpoint, is that you can do it without using much fuel at all; you're just transferring some momentum from one asteroid to another. It would be an amazing feat of engineering, but it does seem within the realm of the possible. Unfortunately, if anyone did it, they could just as easily drop a rock on Earth. On the plus side, Earth has enough atmosphere to burn up most rocks in this size range. Hopefully we won't need to worry about that.

Tom Jolly

Damn the Asteroids, Full Speed Ahead!

Damn the Asteroids, Full Speed Ahead!

Captain Markus Halsey stared in dismay at the dense, careening field of asteroids on the display screen. His Chief Scientist, Obu sub-Abu, shook his head. "They're smacking into each other constantly. Look at how close they are!"

The Captain frowned and nodded. "All moving, and only a few hundred meters between each one. How does a field like this come into existence?"

Obu hacked up a hairball to show his irritation and spit it into a ceramic cup that the Jarn carried for just such a purpose. "Short answer? It can't. If the gormbukking asteroids are banging into each other that often, breaking up all the time, the field is going to get wider as the kinetic energy is distributed and the outer edges expand. The objects will slow down as the impact energy becomes heat, too. Over just a few years, a dense asteroid field like this will be so spread out and the energies so averaged out that the rocks will barely be in view of each other, and for the most part, all headed in the same direction." He shrugged. "Or it's dense enough to coalesce into a planet, and the planet would sweep up most of the loose bits. Either way, it can't last."

Their ship had parked over a hundred kilometers from the outer edge of the vast field, and just in the time they'd sat there, the field had expanded toward them by a good five kilometers. Even now, the number of impacts was falling.

"We were supposed to fly through this crap?" the Captain asked.

"That's what High Command told us," the Chief Pilot said. "There's some new planet we're supposed to explore on the other side. If we want to stay on schedule, we'll have to fly through while the rocks are still spinning around and slamming into everything."

"But if we just wait a day..."

"Then all the rocks will be a few kilometers away from each other. You'll really irritate High Command, though."

Captain Halsey rubbed his chin. "Yeah...we can tell them we had a loose engine belt or something. How long do you suppose this asteroid field has been there?"

"Running the action backwards? I'd say about thirty minutes, sir. The only time I've ever seen asteroids this thick and fast is in some of those ridiculous movies you Earthlings used to eat up," Obu said.

This, the Captain thought, coming from a guy who hacked up hairballs. He scowled at Obu. "Thirty minutes? That's... impossible!"

The Mordu Cleric on the bridge spoke, "This merely adds to the other twenty-nine Incidences of Simulation." It was part of the Mordu religious belief that all creatures were living in a simulation created by a higher-dimensional civilization. Sub-cults within the religion suggested that they were part of a video game, reality show, or some vast experiment. One of the other Incidences was the strange fact that all intelligent creatures looked about the same. No plasma forms, gas bags, or tentacled monsters; it was almost like their Creator had a small budget to work with. Also there was the bizarre coincidence that their technological levels all appeared to be within hundreds of years of one another, despite evolving thousands of light years apart. The list was long.

"Well," said the Captain, "let's just wait it out then. When the cloud of rubble expands far enough to be safe..."

Alarms sounded. "Captain," the First Mate said, "a Ralad Attack Vessel has just appeared on our port bow upper quad. It appears to be powering up its MegaBeam. Our only possible escape is to run through the asteroid field and hope we can dodge all the asteroids."

The Mordu Cleric started laughing.

Some author notes about "Damn the Asteroids..."

I don't write much satire or humor, and this story obviously pokes fun at the movie and TV trope of the "dense asteroid field," along with a few other tropes. Visual stunning, but not very realistic in most cases. Movie makers have been dealing with the problem of realism versus entertainment in SF for a long time, and I don't expect that to change.

Since this is a flash fiction piece, it might seem peculiar to name the entire book after it, but of all the stories, it had the catchiest title, so it won out.

The Mathematician

Cilketat extended an appendage of bodies to Poptikka to establish a closed conversation. Electrical impulses, mind-to-mind, would keep their neighbors from overhearing their conversation, though communicating this way was unintentionally more intimate than audible signals or scents. There was the inevitable likelihood that some bodies would pass between the two of them during the conversation.

It was a much larger mass than Poptikka, having collected, controlled, and fed over two hundred thousand bodies, each six-legged unit contributing its tiny mind to the whole, electrical impulses flitting down the legs to the other units, a perpetually moving mass of bodies the size of small seeds. Parts of it drifted away from the main mass to retrieve bits of fruit and vegetables in the eatery, returning to the main mass only by remembering a pheromonic signature keyed to their tiny minds.

"I need more bodies, Cilketat said. "Smart bodies. I

am close to a breakthrough, I think."

Hundreds of Poptikka's external bodies glanced nervously around the eatery with beetle eyes to see if anyone was paying attention to them, their quiet information transmitted along the strings of a few thousand writhing tiny beetle bodies between them.

"There are tests," it said, "filters you can use to reduce the number of less-able bodies you carry with you. You can select your bodies for certain characteristics, you know. Not just accept the random elements of mixing parties."

"Mixing parties take your soul away."

"Soul!" Poptikka's bodies jerked apart from Cilketat's tendril momentarily, so disgusted was it with the perversion. But, it needed the business, and forced itself to reconnect. The idea that someone would be so committed to retaining its current set of bodies, never replacing the aging units with fresh ones, slowly consuming itself as the bodies died—it made it sick. "You will not find new patterns without mixing. Our whole society would become nothing but..." A group of ten bodies extended from Poptikka's mass, creating a narrow tendril that pointed at a single beetle chewing on a leaf. A loner that lost its primary body. "Losing the self means gaining the knowledge of patterns."

Cilketat released a small puff of noxious odor through one of its tiny bodies. "How many times have we 'learned a new pattern' and then lost the knowledge because of a mixing? Are we just learning the same patterns over and over? I have a pattern of bodies fixed in my core that lets me see numbers in a new way. If I mix now, or ever again, I will lose that pattern."

Poptikka sighed, a hiss of wings rustling on the outer surface of its mass. "That is a perversion many of you science-types share. You think and think, and you waste your body away, close to the next great discovery, until there are no bodies left to feed you. Unaware, you starve to death without realizing that your thoughts have become weak, never translating or transmitting your last great wisdom." An extra impulse of acerbic sarcasm, sharp legs jittering, accompanied its comment.

"I can feed the core. I've configured it with passageways to feed the mass, with caretakers to monitor the bodies."

Poptikka remembered the last mixing party that spawned this version of Cilketat, a group of science-types swapping bodies, purifying ideas, caretaker bodies seething around masses of clarified bodies. A soul, indeed. What narcissism would cause a thinking Keltki to believe itself so important that it would no longer meld with others?

"A filter requires new bodies. Smaller entities, single purpose worker groups, can be encouraged to enter the filter; the units that come out successfully can merge with you. You can even filter your self if you find the mass too ungainly to care for adequately."

Cilketat's surface surged with mild anger at the suggestion it was already overly massive, though it was true. Filtering itself might be worth it to attain its goal.

Near the mat of branches they rested upon, a cluster

of worker-bodies carried grapes past their podra, the layers of soft woven fibers that held their masses. They both sent bodies out to collect some small grapes, exchanging coded electrical signals to provide payment to the eatery. Outside, a web of charged wires glowed white-hot as some predator met its surface. Many of the beetle-bodies glanced up at it, wondering if some crisped body part would fall through the mesh to the eatery floor. By convention, this was food they didn't have to pay for.

Poptikka hissed a sigh. "I know a Kelt who has filters. If you go there, it may help you. Its name is Sheshatak, and it lives within a tree on the eastern edge of this forest. Here is the smell of its place." it puffed a copy of the odor to Cilketat. "Let me warn you; do not choose this path. You will destroy yourself."

"I must go where my mind leads."

"Your mind is everyone's mind. We all share, changing a little at each mixing. We are all immortal."

"Is immortality so valuable? Must knowledge be so transient?"

Poptikka jerked away from Cilketat, hoping that it hadn't somehow been infected with such insanity. The intimate physical connection gone, it vibrated out loud to communicate. "Do what you will, Cilketat. But do not contact me again. Not in this mixing."

The mass of beetles that made up Poptikka's mindbody moved out of the podra to the club's exit. Sheshatak would certainly help Cilketat filter its bodies to purge the less mathematically inclined bits from the mass, to excise the weak-minded entities. But what horror would be left? Poptikka knew that it would have to report this to the counselors; there would be the proof they needed if they caught them in the act of filtering, enough to validate a forced mixing.

Cilketat's massive body shifted from a relatively mindless moving-mode travelling across the forest floor to stationary mind. Its thoughts took form, and it looked up at the large oak tree, eyeing the ornately lined entry to Sheshatak's abode. Finely designed ceramic tiles encircled the hole, and a charged net to ward off predators hung above it. Birds, spiders, and other creatures weren't really deadly; they rarely consumed more than a few bodies, and were often overwhelmed or scared away by the massive numbers of beetles in their bodies, but the net helped when singletons and small groups were sent on tasks from the main body.

It sent a few bodies coded with pheromones into Sheshatak's domain, and after a minute was welcomed in by Sheshatak's own bodies. Its body stretched again into a long, thin mass, climbing into the decorated hollow of the tree.

"Sheshatak. Thank you for seeing me."

"Cilketat. I am not familiar with you."

"Poptikka sent me. It told me you know much about filters. I seek to acquire a purer mind, in order to understand certain mathematical ideas that have been forming within my own."

"Ah," it said. A curious rustling of legs and wings filled the air, and its body nervously backed away from

Cilketat. "Poptikka and I share little in common. Our opinions in most matters diverge. So I'm a little surprised that he, of all collections, should send you to me."

"I used to know Poptikka well, many mixings ago, but I believe we no longer agree on some of the most fundamental aspects on maintaining self. The purification of one's mind, and maintenance of its state. I am depending on its past companionship. It remembers me, I think, fondly, and offered me this last favor before we parted ways."

"Self. That is a very dangerous subject." Sheshatak considered this, the soft hush of crawling and twitching bodies betraying only deep thought. "I can do this," it said. "It will not be free, you know."

"Of course not. I have funds available for this."

"Then let me show you the filters." Sheshatak led Cilketat down a narrow tube of natural wood deeper into the tree's body. A complex weave of thin copper wire in a confusion of patterns was inlaid into the walls of the tube. Sheshatak admired them. A thin layer of epoxy prevented the wood from growing out around the pattern of wire, its odor overwhelming the natural smells of Sheshatak's home.

In the open hollow there were a number of small wooden and metal devices with entries and exits. Some of the exits were attached to tubes that led to the wall of the tree, exiting to the outside. *Where the rejects go,* Cilketat thought. Sheshatak pointed to one of the smallest. "This one is the simplest, for single bodies, containing a one-way passage and a lever. Each body is asked to figure out their way through this tube. It is very basic, and is merely a filter to weed out parasitic bodies that do little but feed and excrete. Some entities think that these are the core of our body's personality, physically useless but shaping what we are and how we think. Philosopher bodies, if you will." Its mass twitched back and forth, a sign of doubt. "From there, the filters become more complex; mazes based on logic that require body clusters of at least ten units, visual perception filters, puzzles and paths of verbal comprehension, riddles that test the tiny mind of a microcluster."

"I need something very special. I have a strong core of mathematical skills, a fixed mesh of bodies highly skilled in that one area. What I need are bodies who can find the synergistic connections between a diverse spectrum of ideas; the genius that can find linkages that open up higher tiers of thought."

"You wish to increase the neural connectivity of your bodies. To increase understanding."

"I believe that is so." Cilketat's body hissed and twitched in anticipation. It could barely contain the vibrating beetles within itself.

"We will need to create a baseline with your existing clusters, perhaps twenty to thirty units each, then...what's that?" A hundred beetle eyes focused on a lone body coming out of one of the filters. "A wanderer has found it's way in through a filter." Sheshatak sent out a group to shoo it away, back out the main tunnel above, but then another and another came in through other filter exits. "This is highly unusual," it squeaked.

In a matter of seconds, the chamber was flooded with other bodies, a river of beetles tumbling, rolling, crawling down the tube above and pouring in through the filter exits. They formed up into new bodies as they came in. Cilketat and Sheshatak both recognized the odors. "The council!" Sheshatak cried. "We are unmade!"

"Poptikka has betrayed me! Betrayed us!"

Sheshatak spread out, trying to find any way out, but found itself blocked at every exit by council bodies, its probes failing, finally reassembling with wings and legs flailing and rubbing, screaming out, "Foolish Cilketat! Poptikka is not like us! It changes at every mixing! You cannot trust one that changes itself constantly."

"Obscenity and perversion!" one of the council shouted. "Listen; they condemn themselves! Mix them, unmake them! We cannot let such monstrosities as these abide."

All the bodies in the core of the old oak seethed together, pushing forcefully into the writhing bodies of Cilketat and Sheshatak, flowing and churning and twisting, a tornado of tiny brown carapaces. One mass held together as though it was one solid unit, a sphere of solidity in the maelstrom, a symmetric core of being, rolling to a stop as the main bodies of the council reformed, both of the renegades absorbed within them.

Benoltba shuddered as the units of its body settled into a partially new configuration, random new thoughts twisted amongst its own. Where perversion appeared, it reorganized the clusters so they no longer held together, assuring that only the utility of their single bodies, and not the sparks of settled thought, remained behind. In minutes, the riotous noise of scraping legs and rattled wings settled into a susurration of quiet thought. Benoltba spoke. "They are gone."

"They are gone, and yet still part of each of us," echoed the council member Aratskat. it shuddered at the thought, but this formality of closure was met. "But what is this that remains behind?"

The council members gathered around a strange sphere of beetles, sparking and twitching, but unmoving. Tunnels of darkness riddled the sphere, tunnels they recognized would be necessary to feed the static mass of intricately and tightly connected bodies. "It was in Cilketat's very core. It must have carried it. Why would it carry such a doomed object? Wouldn't the bodies die?"

"In years, perhaps. Maybe the filters would have given it the tools to maintain it."

"But...what is it? I have seen tool-bodies before, ten or twenty large, created for a single purpose, but this is huge. It cannot be..."

Aratskat reached out a link of bodies to touch the object, electrical impulses traveling between them. "Ah—" it said. The other councilors back up cautiously. Dozens of bodies within Aratskat clicked amusement. "It – it adds!" it rustled anxiously, holding the connection. "It multiplies!" It detached its bodies and spun in excitement. "It is a math machine! The core of Cilketat was a calculation device!"

"So, another abomination. We should destroy it."

"No!" Aratskat cried out. "This is not self, not

149

narcissism, not a creature bent on avoiding the mix of life! It is a tool, like the digger clusters we create, or the carriers and harvesters, an unthinking tool to use."

Benoltba stared with a hundred eyes, trying to penetrate the thing. "A calculator. Cilketat sought self because of a tool it thought was part of itself. It thought a tool was its own heart."

"But it created this tool." Aratskat asked itself, *Is there then value in self? Or only as a transition to create new tools for the mixed? How many other tools have arisen this way?*

"It did. All Keltki can use this tool now, or copy its structure. Perhaps they can create variations that will work in other useful ways. We need not discard a useful tool just because it was spawned by the obscenity of self."

A calculator! How many tools have come from a body bent on purifying a single idea, where the idea was of such a value as to risk maintaining self to keep it alive? Aratskat wondered, twisted clusters of Cilketat and Sheshatak already working their magic on it, tumbled bodies of untried concepts, twitching connections of altered philosophies straining at the foundations of its beliefs.

Aratskat rustled wings and legs, but remained silent. Some thoughts could not be shared.

Some Author Notes for "The Mathematician"

This story was actually a spin-off from my short story "Cradle" that was published in 2015 in Daily Science Fiction. There, I introduced seven alien species that were about as alien as I could justifiably make them, and after a year or so of having these weird species milling about in my head, I wondered, how would a colonial beetle species actually exist? How would the transient nature of its so-called brain cells affect its life cycle? Or more importantly, its philosophy and society? One thing led to another, and here you have it. Essentially immortality, with the understanding that some of your memories might be eaten by a crow on occasion.

Tom Jolly

The First Shot Fired

"The planet is about twenty-four light years from Earth. From what we can tell from here, it's got water and free oxygen, and it's in the sun's habitable zone. It's very promising, sir."

"And it's called Gliese?"

"Gliese 667Cc. The naming committee has tentatively come up with 'Vogt's World', after one of the scientists who discovered it."

"And you think we should fund a mission to it?"

Henderson shrugged. "A probe. Nothing spectacular. Take some photos, gather a little spectral data, transmit it back. If there's plant life, or even just bacteria growing there, we'll be able to detect it. But it's going to need some leading-edge tech to communicate its findings from twenty-four light years away. And to get there within our lifetimes."

President Cochran smiled. "Well, my doctor says I'm

likely good to 140, and I'm only seventy now, so that shouldn't be a problem. Twenty-four years isn't that long."

"No, sir, that's twenty-four light years. It's a distance, not a time. With our best tech, it'll take forty years to get there, without slowing down once we arrive. It'd be a fly-by. And once it gets there, another twenty-four years for any data to return, moving at light-speed."

The President's brow furrowed. "So if I understand you right, that's what? Sixty-four years? That'll be a hard sell to the American public. What sort of cost are we talking about?"

"Maybe ten billion, plus or minus a few billion in pocket change. A big chunk of that is for the modified ground-based lasers stationed around the world that can be reused for other light-sail missions. We've got a top-secret mod to reduce beam divergence to near zero, so we can maintain thrust at a half-gee for almost eighteen months, though we won't be telling the public about that. But we can pitch the ground-based installations as an innovative reusable laser-launch system that anyone can use, and develop the long-range light-sail probe on the side. It'll look cheap in comparison."

The President tapped his teeth with a pen, thinking. "Well, let's label it as a defense system so we can sell it to both sides of the aisle," he said. "Do we have the tech we need?"

"The solar sail and the ground-based lasers are proven hardware. As for the rest of it, I've brought Dr. Shamut, here, to explain the new tech required."

President Cochran nodded at the other man seated in the room, and said, "My next meeting is in five minutes, so try to keep it simple for me."

Shamut smiled nervously, running his hand through dark and unruly hair. He clearly wasn't used to visiting anyone but his engineering staff. "Well, to start we have to engineer the solar sail material so it can switch from clear to opaque. This should not be difficult, since such transition materials are commonly used as films on windows, but it will increase the weight of the solar sail. When the probe is very far from here, we select a trajectory that puts it between the Earth and Gliese 667C once a year, thus blocking a small fraction of the light from that sun. Then, we use a tiny bit of power to wink the solar sail on and off, either blocking Gliese's rays, or letting them through. It eliminates the need for a high-powered transmitter. We use the power of Gliese 667C to power our communications."

"Brilliant!" the President exclaimed, eyes glazed like a china doll. "And that will provide communications from twenty-some light years away?"

Shamut and Henderson exchanged a hesitant glance, which immediately put the President on alert. Shamut clasped his hands together, and said, "Well, not exactly. When we get close enough to gather visual data, the probe will no longer be between the star and us. However, we have a technology loosely based on ferroliquids that will let us disperse a large cloud of ionized particles in space and shape them with a magnetic field. This can be used as a giant low-frequency antenna with which to transmit data back to Earth once the probe arrives."

The President sniffed, as though trying to ferret out a rotten egg. "Okay. So far that doesn't sound too bad. What is it you're not telling me?"

Henderson butted in. "Sir, we need a shaped tactical-nuclear device. If the ferrocloud disperses slowly, the solar winds will trash it before we can shape it and use it. We need to use a very powerful, precisely designed explosive to disperse the particle cloud fast enough and widely enough to be of use to us as a high-gain radio antenna."

President Cochran rolled his eyes. "So what you're actually telling me is that you want part of the probe design to be run as a covert project?"

They both nodded.

The President sat back and drummed his fingers on the desk. He glanced at his watch. "Time for my next meeting. You'll have to excuse me." He stood and shook Shamut's hand. "Generally, Dr. Shamut, I like the idea and I think we can move forward with this. Work out the details with Henderson, and please keep me informed on the status."

From Vogt's World, locally known as Pru, Vogt-1's solar sail looked like a tiny star headed for their solar system. The *pruins* knew forty years before that the probe was headed their way; they'd heard about it from Earth broadcasts. And they'd been arguing continuously as to whether they should let the probe arrive or not.

"The humans are not ready to contact the Twelve. Even now, there are six wars continuing on Earth. Their news is rife with murder, conflict, and the destruction of their own ecosystem."

"Well, they do have their downsides, I'll admit. But they had the technology and curiosity send this probe out."

The *pruin* snorted, his *loquin* quivering in disdain. "So did the Hive Machines back in 60601, but that did not make it acceptable for them to join the rest of us."

Another *borbolled* in agreement. "The universe would likely be a safer place without the potential threat of the humans."

"You aren't seriously suggesting removing humans from the *shozbat* pool merely because of what they *might* do in the future?"

"Why not? Humans are apparently quite good at killing off imaginary threats before they become actual threats."

"So we should lower our standards to that of humans?"

One *pruin*, larger than the rest, slapped his *palak* on the table. "This isn't a moral discussion about eliminating humans, we just need to decide whether to destroy their cursed probe or not."

"We will regret letting the humans survive. Mark my words."

The bureaucrats, as many do, continued to rail at each other while postponing any decision or action. The probe entered their solar system and started recording data. They adjourned for their four-hour lunch break. By the time they returned, it would be far too late to do anything about the probe.

All species harbor a few specimens who are willing to go down to the beach to watch a tidal wave. Lepranik and Varprasil had taken a day-jaunt to Shinpru, one of the moons off Lamuth, a gas giant four orbits out from Pru. The crawling gardens of Shinpru were known throughout the Twelve. But Lepranik had other ideas once they reached space.

"Let's visit that Earthling probe!" he suggested, shading his *labut* to olive-green, indicating a level of excitement mixed with anxiety.

Varprasil curled his *loquin* in disapproval. "The council has not yet decided if the probe should be destroyed or not."

"The council couldn't make a decision in a full orbit, even if it concerned putting out a fire on their moldy gray *labuts*. The probe has passed its closest approach to Pru, and if it hasn't finished taking pictures, I'm sure it's going to very soon." Lepranik shifted the lever on the quantum equivalence relocator and transferred their quantum stats to a nexus near the probe. "Where's the light sail?"

"It detached from the probe shortly after the probe left their heliosphere to reduce interstellar drag. You can see the probe on the monitor, though." Vaprasil pointed to a glowing dot hovering in the map-space between them. "It's very small. He peered at the map-space as the glowing dot split apart. "Now there are two pieces. One is drifting away from the other." He leaned back, his *loquin* shaking nervously. "We shouldn't be here," he muttered.

"Pah. Let's get closer. It's only moving at point-seven light." Lepranik flipped on the lightwarper to make sure they appeared invisible to the probe's cameras, then tweaked the control lever again to match vectors. A few gentle adjustments got them within ten meters of the smaller probe section.

"Not much to it," Vaprasil said.

"This part of it would fit in our cargo bay, don't you think? We could grab it, pop over to Earth tonight, drop it in their orbit, and be back before *zutch*. Wouldn't they be surprised!"

"I think the council would cut off our *drassils* for such a stunt. You know we're under a strict mandate to avoid contact with humans." He stared at the probe. "Fortunate for us that we haven't used radio waves for over 50,000 years."

"Let's grab it anyway. In a big city like ours, we could get top creds for a human artifact."

Vaprasil chuckled. "Well! I do believe you are correct. However, humans may be curious if their probe suddenly stops broadcasting data."

"Pah. It's well past perigee. I'm sure it's done taking data by now. They'll never notice."

Molnidoss had a reputation in the alien artifact and fossil business, along with a sideline of contraband living biospecimens. His storefront gaudily displayed the legal half of the business, but they were mostly items that could be had from a dozen such dealers across the city. The advantage of living in the largest city on Pru, despite the competition, was the ready access to a wide base of customers who wanted something unique. Something that the law might frown upon.

Vaprasil and Lepranik had business on the marginal side of legal with Molnidoss in the past. They brought the human satellite into Molnidoss' warehouse on a floater and proudly displayed it for him, waiting for an estimate.

"You're in luck," Molnidoss told them. "When you contacted me, I called a client who already has some interest in human artifacts."

"Here in Varsanika?"

"No, hundreds of drik from here," Molnidoss said, evasively. The two of them, he knew, were just the types to try to circumvent him as the middleman. "Let me scan this for pathogens. You'll get less if I have to sterilize it first, and a lot less if it makes me sick with some *polotni* bug."

He grabbed the scanner from a storage shelf and stared at the 3D display that popped up above it, positioning it to see the entire satellite. "Hmm. No biologicals. Plenty of radiation."

Vaprisil nodded. "The humans use radioactive materials with thermal converters to provide long-duration power. They use it whenever they send a probe far from the sun."

Molnidoss pointed at a tube-shaped device. "That explains this bit. What about this cluster over here?"

They leaned forward, peering through the layers of

holographic imagery. Molnidoss frowned. "You did disconnect the power before you brought this thing in, didn't you?" They heard something click, and for a very brief moment, watched as a dozen small squibs exploded, driving packets of plutonium together, and Molnidoss used the last fraction of a second of his life considering how disappointed his customer would be that his Earth artifact was no longer available, and whether he'd complain to the authorities about it.

Ex-President Cochran sat on the porch in his retirement home in Avila Beach. He was celebrating his 110th birthday, and his old friend Henderson had come to visit.

"Vogt-1 will have started transmitting its first photos back by now," Cochran said.

Henderson nodded. "And all we have to do is wait twenty-four years to see if the planet is habitable. I hope I live long enough to see that day."

They sat and watched the evening sky, celebrating his birthday with thirty-year-old Glenmorangie and comfortable silence stirred by a warm ocean breeze. Stars began to appear, and then more stars, and more stars. The sky became dense with tiny lights, and then they all began to move.

"Now that's odd," Cochran said.

Henderson stared in disbelief at the sky. Memories from forty years before poured unbidden into his mind, and it only took moments for him to guess what had happened. Momentarily, he thought about what faster-than-light flight could mean for humanity. If any of them were still alive by tomorrow. He bent his head down and closed his eyes, a tear trying to escape from one corner, but he rubbed it away before it could morph into an actual emotion. What use was that now? Sighing, he stood up, picked up the bottle of Scotch and topped off both their glasses, then sat back down to watch the show.

Some author notes on "The First Shot Fired"

I was pondering the problem of interstellar communication from a small probe, and how it might expend very little power to communicate by using the target star's own rays, intermittently blocking them to send a signal. That was the seed for the story, and I was kind of proud of the idea. Once the probe gets to the star, though, the ability to communicate by "winking a shield on and off" goes away, and I introduced the nuke, and the rest of the story just fell into place.

Gliese 667Cc was picked as a target planet when it looked promising, but I don't think it's quite as attractive anymore. The problem with SF is that new data comes in so fast nowadays that by the time a story is accepted and published, the science behind it is often out-of-date. Reality is changing faster than we can make stuff up.

Tom Jolly

Star Drive

Busar Kioko carefully turned up the air pressure on the breathing air, far away from the Honda Fit automobile. A thirty foot line fed the air from the tank to a valve welded onto the side of the Honda. Ayo Mwangi crouched next to Busar, behind a thick piece of plywood. "What happened the first time you tried this?" Ayo asked.

"The front wind shield popped out at twenty-two PSI," Busar said. "It landed on Mari's corn, and she was very angry with me."

Ayo looked over his shoulder at the beat-up car. Busar had welded steel rods over the outer surface of the car's windows, like jail bars, with rubber pads underneath each bar so that the windows wouldn't crack as they pushed against the bars. "The car's windows appear to be designed to keep pressure out instead of in," Busar continued. He looked down at his gage. "We are at thirty PSI. Over two atmospheres!"

"And that is the same as being in space at one atmosphere?"

"Yes, of course," Busar said. He stood up and

walked over to the car, which was hissing loudly. "There are still a lot of small leaks. I welded the biggest holes. These cars float very well, for a while, even if you don't fill in all the holes, so they are mostly airtight. If you teleport the car into space, then you will still need a tank of air, though, and I doubt that it would last more than a half-hour."

Ayo joined him and put his hands on his hips, staring critically at the ugly, patchwork thing. "You should have started from scratch. It would look better."

Busar waved his hand at the monster. "This was cheap. No engine!"

When he was very young, Ayo had learned he could teleport himself and the things he touched, and nearly crushed some houses with a large boulder by accident. He became more cautious as the years went by, hiding his ability as it got him into more and more trouble. He was even accused of being a witch. His actions caused dangerous people to come looking for him, though it didn't keep him from doing fast transports for certain customers, especially if borders were a problem. It put food on the table.

But the edge of space, where the air became too thin, had always been a problem for him. He never made enough money to buy an actual space suit; the more transports he performed, the more notorious and visible he became, and the more likely he was to be trapped or killed by some nefarious and enterprising villain.

He enlisted the aid of his childhood friend, Busar

Kioko, to help him create a tiny spaceship. One with no rockets, no radio, no air recycler, and no computer. What Busar told Ayo was this; "A rocket should be made out of metal, and for yours, you will need windows so you can see where you are going. We will start with a car, and modify it for space."

And now they had one.

Busar and Ayo sat in the front seat of the car, looking through the vertical bars welded across the windshield at the rusty hood, and beyond that, weeds and rocks and dirt. Busar was in the driver's seat for no other reason than he wanted to pretend he was driving the car into space. At the small shack they kept for these remote tests away from prying eyes, Abo's wife Mari waved at the two of them, expecting them both back for lunch. They had done crazier things than this before.

"Are you ready?" Ayo asked.

"I…" Busar said, and then they were one hundred kilometers high, looking down on the Earth in their flying Honda.

Busar gasped, his eyes widened, and both hands were white-knuckled as he gripped the steering wheel. The car immediately began to fall in the vacuum, and the two of them felt their stomachs lurch.

"Are we in orbit?" Busar asked.

Ayo had been reading a bit about orbits and flying in space since Busar started welding supporting structure onto the car and said, "No, I sent us straight up. Now we are just falling down. To be in orbit, we have to go very fast around the Earth."

"How fast?" Busar asked.

"It depends on how high we are. If we orbit close to the Earth, we need to go around the Earth at over seven kilometers per second. But I have no reference to measure that just using my eyes." He looked out the window of the car through the self-adhesive polarized sun screen attached to the window, wondering if they might get a sunburn. It felt very warm. He teleported the car to rotate it, so the bottom was facing the sun.

The right side window was filled with a view of a giant blue marble, the reflected light dimly illuminating the inside of the car. Busar pointed and said, "Is that Kenya?"

Ayo nodded. "The border lines seem to be missing," he joked.

Excitedly, Busar said, "Look! A satellite," as a dot of light flashed past them.

"I can use it as a reference to put us into orbit," Ayo said, and as quickly as a thought, the car was flitting alongside the spacecraft. The satellite appeared to be little more than a cylinder with solar panels adhered to its side, and a small antenna sticking out one end, surrounded by a cluster of other unrecognizable instruments.

"I do not recognize the satellite," Busar said.

"I would not recognize any satellite," Ayo replied.

In awe, they watched the pearlescent oceans and clouds rotate below them for a while, commenting on various landmarks they thought they recognized, until Busar pointed at a small red dot in the sky. "Is that

Mars?"

"I think it is. Should I try to jump there?" Ayo suggested.

"How far can you jump?"

Ayo shrugged, and suddenly they were much closer to the red dot. It was difficult to judge distance in space. "It is strange," Ayo said. "The Earth still looks very close. Let me just…" and then they jumped again, instantly closing the gap to the red dot.

"What!" Busar shouted, seeing a brilliant red sports car coming at him at a meter per second from only a few meters away, and he stomped on his brakes, jerked the steering wheel sideways, and honked the horn, which barely sounded through the frame to the inside the Honda, and then they ran into the only other car that was within a hundred thousand kilometers of them. The other driver, in a space suit, lurched forward in his seat with the impact, but they both only hit on a fender, and a few moments later Ayo had gathered his wits about him and relocated their car. Through a number of quick jumps he dumped their orbital velocity and brought the car back down to their dusty retreat in Kenya.

Busar sat in the driver's seat still gripping the steering wheel, shaking. Ayo stared at him, concerned, then slowly broke into a smile and started laughing. Busar turned red and stuttered, "What is so funny?"

"You put on the brakes! And the horn!" He continued laughing.

"Why was there a car in space? That is ridiculous." Busar grumbled and shook his head, then saw Mari motioning to them from the front stoop of the shack. "Teleport us out of this deathtrap and let's go eat lunch."

A few thousand miles away a very rich man watched a video playback with his hand over his mouth, shaking his head at the image of two crazed men, one clutching the top of the dashboard, the other trying to steer his car in a vacuum, both clearly screaming, though no sound could be heard from the recording. The car swept out of camera range, and then couldn't be found again.

The rich man leaned back in his chair and rubbed his face. "What did I just see?" he asked.

"Sir," his assistant replied, "we aren't entirely sure."

After a while, he said, "Do you think my insurance…"

"Not a chance. Sir."

Some author notes on "Star Drive"

This story snippet was part of a series of stories about Ayo, the teleporter. I don't actually remember why I chose to put this in Kenya, and more than once have considered moving the entire set of stories to the US where I'm more familiar with the culture, but Ayo and Busar have grown on me. I like them and want to explore their characters and motivations and learn more about their culture, so I've taken to reading a few books by Kenyan authors.

The end of the story is about the red Tesla automobile that Elon Musk sent up into space, if that isn't clear to my readers. I sent the story to one magazine only a matter of months after Elon Musk performed that stunt, and it was rejected in part because the end of the story confused the editor; he had no idea what I was talking about.

Anyway…if Ayo and Busar seem interesting to you, let me know. I'm well into writing a book about the two of them, and would love to hear that people are interested in their odd story.

Tom Jolly

For more short stories and updates, please visit
http://www.silcom.com/~tomjolly/tomjolly2.htm

To contact the author, email
tomjolly@silcom.com

Follow @tomjolly19 on twitter.

ABOUT THE AUTHOR

Tom Jolly is a retired astronautical/electrical engineer who now spends his time writing SF and fantasy, designing board games, and creating obnoxious puzzles. His stories have appeared in Analog SF, Daily Science Fiction, Compelling Science Fiction, New Myths, and a number of anthologies, including "As Told By Things" and "Shards". He lives in Santa Maria, California, with his wife Penny in a place where mountain lions and black bears still visit.

If you enjoyed this book, consider looking at "The Witch and the Two-Headed Boy", another collection of short stories, and "An Unusual Practice," about a human doctor that unexpectedly finds himself treating a community of supernatural creatures. Both books are available on Amazon.

Made in the USA
Las Vegas, NV
26 October 2021